S0-DTD-227
ELMORE

Alone with Shaw, your traveling companion, in an unmapped chamber of the Caves of Gallendale, you are suddenly threatened on all sides by a horde of ugly goblins.

As one of the filthy creatures tries to grab you, Shaw shouts, "Don't touch her!" and swings his sword in a great arc, knocking several weapons from goblin hands. Badly outnumbered, he bravely continues to flail his sword while you search for an exit.

A spell would work, you think. You could draw on your secret powers as a magic-user and cast a spell to distract the goblins long enough for you both to escape.

Yes, a spell would work, you think, *work to ruin the relationship building between Shaw and me.* Your heart pounds with fear—fear of the horrible goblins, and fear of losing Shaw by revealing yourself as a sorceress.

The creatures are overwhelming Shaw. You must act!

Will you cast a spell to distract the goblins
and, thereby, reveal your true identity to Shaw?
If so, turn to page 123.

Or will you take up one of the goblins' fallen weapons
and join Shaw in the fight?
If this is your choice, turn to page 154.

Whichever path you pick, you are sure to find romance and adventure as the SECRET SORCERESS

Have you read these
HEARTQUEST™ adventure-romance books?

#1 RING OF THE RUBY DRAGON

#2 TALISMAN OF VALDEGARDE

#3 SECRET SORCERESS

#4 ISLE OF ILLUSION

#3

Secret Sorceress

BY LINDA LOWERY

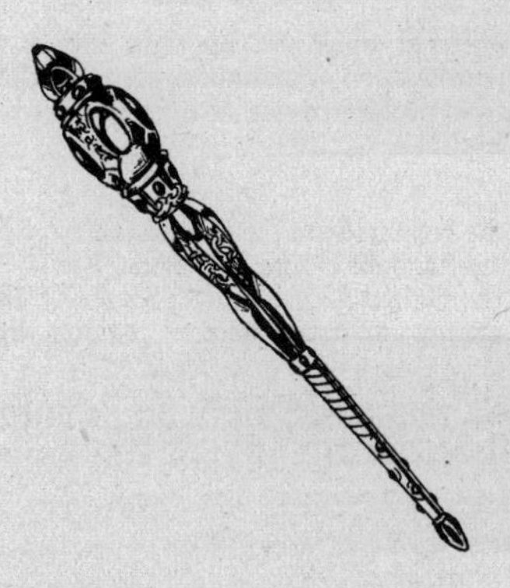

Cover art by Elmore
Interior art by Jim Holloway

TSR, Inc.
PRODUCTS OF YOUR IMAGINATION™

For June Hadley,
a sorceress of fine powers

SECRET SORCERESS

Distributed to the book trade in the United States by Random House, Inc. and in Canada by Random House of Canada, Ltd.
Distributed in the United Kingdom by TSR (UK), Ltd.
Distributed to the toy and hobby trade by regional distributors.

First Printing: November, 1983
Printed in he United States of America.
Library of Congress Catalog Card Number: 83-51037
ISBN: 0-88038-067-5

9 8 7 6 5 4 3 2 1

TSR, Inc.
P.O. Box 756
Lake Geneva, WI 53147

TSR (UK), Ltd.
The Mill, Rathmore Road
Cambridge CB1 4AD
United Kingdom

You are about to set off on a romantic adventure in which *you* will face many decisions. Some choices you will determine with your head—others with your heart. Each choice takes you on a different path to a separate ending. So be careful . . . you must choose wisely!

Do not read this book from beginning to end. Instead, as you are faced with a decision, follow the instructions and keep turning to the pages to which your choices lead you until you come to an end. You may meet a handsome adventurer or chance upon self-discovery. Success or disaster—the choice that leads you there is yours!

I am so tired," you complain, rolling over to see who's bothering you. "And I know it's not time to—" You sit upright, pulling the covers up around your neck. There, perched on your bedpost, is a goldfinch, a parchment scroll dangling from her beak.

"Who are you?" you demand. "And just what are you doing in my room?"

"The wizard Junius sent me," answers the bird. "He died last night in prison, and his last command was to deliver this scroll to you at once."

"Not Junius!" you cry. "He was the last wizard left in the kingdom!"

"Yes," says the finch, dropping the scroll into your lap. "The Yorguths finally starved him to death."

"I just can't believe Junius is dead," you murmur. You remember visiting him the day the Yorguths stormed into his cottage, ripping apart his belongings until they found his spell book. They tore pages from the book, hurling the crumpled paper in his face. "Magic is evil! And you shall die for your wicked sorcery, wizard!" they growled. You shudder, as you remember shuddering then, helplessly watching the barbarians drag poor Junius off to prison.

"Hurry and read the scroll!" pipes the finch. "It's nearly dawn, and soon Lord Ungaar and his Yorguths will awaken."

You quickly unroll the parchment and read:

Go now to the cavern wall
And trust your powers rare.
The moon at midnight will reveal
Your secret destiny there.

"The Cavern of Enchantment?" you ask, clutching the scroll to your heart.

"Exactly," says the finch. "At the junction of Gallendale and Blissford kingdoms. I've hidden a map for you at the North Willow."

"But if Ungaar discovers I've gone, he'll be enraged. He'll come after me, imprison me, perhaps even kill me. I took the Oath of Fealty years ago, and I owe him my life . . ."

"Fiddle!" snaps the finch. "You have allegiance to much higher powers than that evil barbarian. You must trust the scroll, Mialie. It is the Scroll of Destiny."

"But don't I owe Ungaar something? He raised me from infancy. He found me in a basket in the marsh—"

"So he tells you," interrupts the bird. "But can't you see that he has imprisoned you here, making you toil in the fields from dawn till dusk, like a slave? Believe me, Mialie, you have much to learn about yourself and your true destiny."

You close your eyes, turning the decision over in your mind. Since you can remember, you have always feared and hated the Yorguths, their restrictive laws, their cold-blooded violence. Somehow you always knew you were different, that there was more in store for you.

You leap from your bed. "The cavern it is!" you say, a fluttery feeling rising in your stomach. You slip into your long homespun skirt, and button up the green-gold blouse that matches your eyes. Just as you finish lacing flowers into your hair, you rush to the bed and pull a little black book from under the pillow.

"Your spell book?" asks the finch.

Your grip tightens around the book. "How did you know that?" you ask, eyeing the bird anxiously. "I've never told anyone . . ."

"That you are a sorceress?" pipes the bird. "But Junius knew from the time you were born. Just be cautious about using your magic," warns the finch. "If the Yorguths discover you, your fate will be no better than that of Junius."

"I know," you say, shuddering at speaking of your magic powers aloud. As you leave your cottage, you ask, "What's your name?" hoping to change the subject. But the finch doesn't answer, for you are in the village now, tiptoeing silently past the other cottages.

At the outskirts of the village, you turn to take a last look at Ungaar's castle, a delicate, spired castle that was once the home of the King and Queen of Gallendale. How often you awoke in the dead of night to hear tortured screams echoing from the windows, screams of victims wrongly accused of being evil sorcerers! You shiver and turn away, feeling somehow you will never return to the dreadful existence you have known here.

The finch leads you down a zigzag path, through the blue fog that rises from the tall grasses of the valley.

When you are a safe distance from town, she says, "Worm. Worm's my name."

"Why would a bird be called Worm?" you ask.

"After the Yorguths conquered the kingdom, Junius started calling me Worm. He said I should have the name of a lowly creature, befitting the Yorguth mentality. I even stopped singing. They hate music almost as much as they hate magic, you know."

"And they have no right to be ruling, either, do they?" you ask. "They never found the Scepter of Power. I hear it vanished about the time the King and Queen of Gallendale were executed."

"That's right. And Ungaar shall never find the scepter," Worm says firmly. "He is not the rightful heir to Gallendale. Or Blissford either, for that matter."

She swoops down onto the branch of a willow tree. "Here we are. I left the map in that hole in the . . ." Worm stops abruptly. "Do you see what I see?"

Yes, you do see it. At the base of the willow lies a young man, dressed in garments of silk, his head a halo of blond curls. He is sleeping as though he hasn't a care in the world, with his belongings scattered about him: a mandolin, a jeweled sword, and a small lumpy back-pack. In his hand is a scroll that looks like yours.

"Is that our map in his hand?" you ask Worm.

The sound of your voice wakes him, and his eyes open slowly and dreamily, eyes the color of a pool of water on an overcast day.

"Good morning," he says, running his fingers through tangled curls. "Did you come for this map?"

You are speechless. This man is different, you think. Not at all like the heavy, red-haired Yorguths with their big heads and thick bodies. There is a delicacy in his long limbs, a gentleness in his face.

"We certainly did," snaps Worm, darting over to snatch it from his hand. But he tightens his grasp and smiles a pleasant, easy smile.

"I'm Shaw," he says, rising to his feet. "And here is your map." He places it in your hands and Worm fluffs up her feathers indignantly.

"You could have given it to me," she says. "I'm the official messenger."

"And what, pray tell, is your name?" Shaw asks you, ignoring the bird.

"I am Mialie," you tell him. "And how, may I ask, did you get my map?"

"I was wandering through the valley last night and happened upon this willow tree. Out of pure curiosity, I gazed into the hole, and there I found a map of Blissford and Gallendale, with directions to the cavern. Blissford was my birthplace," he adds. "I am the son of the late king and queen of that kingdom."

Your mouth drops open, and you close it quickly. "You're a prince?" you ask, trying to appear nonchalant.

"I would have been the next King of Blissford, if that's what you mean. But, of course, the Yorguths made sure that no one but Ungaar would rule."

Worm begins to preen herself and flutter about. "So where do you live now?" she asks.

"Everywhere. Anywhere," he answers, slipping his jeweled sword into its sheath. "I'm a wanderer. I just keep out of trouble, traveling from sunrise to sunset, season to season."

"You must know your way around the back country," you say, "if you travel all the time."

"I'd say so," he answers, a wide grin brightening his face. "Does that mean you want me to take you to the cavern? I surely don't need a map to get there."

Can you imagine me, you think, *journeying cross-kingdom with a prince?* You feel your cheeks start to flush. *If he only knew that I'm an orphan, and a witch besides, he'd never want to join me.*

"I haven't anything more important to do," says the prince, "and I'm looking for an adventure. I've heard some wild tales about the Cavern of Enchantment. Did you know that people have been turned to stone there? Some sort of magic must be associated with it."

Your heart goes cold. *He suspects my magic powers,* you think. *And how could he? He only just met me.*

"Thank you for your offer," you say. "But I am perfectly capable of getting to the cavern on my own."

"My, my," says the prince, grinning. "I'm not asking for your hand in marriage, Mialie. I'm just looking for an adventure, and I'm sure my fighting abilities could be helpful to you. You're embarking on a very dangerous journey, you know."

You glare at him, a strange anger rising in you. What nerve he has, speaking of marriage in such an offhand manner. Suddenly, Worm is on your shoulder, whispering, "He's gorgeous, Mialie, and strong, besides. He could charm the feathers off a bird. Tell him to join you."

Your insides are a tangle of emotions. You are enraged that he thinks he's so charming, upset that you feel so inferior, irritated that the goldfinch wants to interfere. But Worm is right. There is something about his easy manner, his confident smile, that shoots straight to your heart. You feel yourself begin to blush, and you quickly unroll the map.

"Even with you along, Prince Shaw, I prefer to follow the map," you say, concentrating hard to force the redness from your cheeks. "Now, the map shows three ways to get to the cavern. We can travel through the Caves of Gallendale, across the Cloistered Valley, or along the Castle River in Blissford."

You glance up to see that Shaw is watching you with amusement, his gray eyes dancing. You feel your face turn red again, and lower your head toward the map.

"The caves look like the quickest route, but I've heard they're crawling with goblins and could be dangerous," you say.

"And the valley is beautiful," adds Worm, "except very close to town. It's probably the first place Ungaar would search for you."

"I know Blissford best of all," says Shaw. "But I must warn you, it's a rather desolate place. The Yorguths have demolished many of the castles along the river by now."

"Well," says Worm, turning to you, "it's your journey. Which way do you want to go?"

Through the Cloistered Valley. Turn to page 41.

Into the Caves of Gallendale. Turn to page 27.

Along the Castle River. Turn to page 15.

"The green dragon is mean, but it's just a baby, as I recall," says Waldemar, leading you through a maze of passageways, between stalagmites and beneath stalactites. "We'll handle him with one hand behind our backs."

"How?" you ask, eager to learn a new spell.

"Let me handle the details," says the wizard. "You just stand back out of my way when we get there."

You and Shaw exchange wary looks, but you continue to follow along until you enter a huge chamber flooded with water. At the far end, guarding the exit, is a green dragon. It is tiny, smaller than you, and looks nothing like the forbidding monster you had envisioned.

"A mere lizard," exclaims Waldemar. "I'd forgotten it was so puny. Wait right here while I handle this."

Just as Waldemar approaches the dragon, an amazing and horrible thing happens. The dragon begins to grow bigger, until, within seconds, it is as tall as the cave, its teeth huge and jagged, its claws like sharpened swords. It lets out a roar that echoes through the chamber and you back up against the wall, trembling.

"And you thought I was still a baby!" snarls the dragon, laughing at Waldemar. "Didn't you know that dragons grow up?"

With a fierce cry, the monster lunges at the wizard, knocking him to the floor of the cave with one hit. It tosses back its scaly head and laughs loudly.

"Waldemar isn't dead," Shaw whispers. "I can see him breathing. He must be unconscious."

The dragon's claws swoop down and clamp the wizard tightly, imprisoning him. It glares at you with demonic eyes, and then its gaze moves to Shaw. The monster stretches its long neck toward him ominously.

"Just give me the sword at your side," it demands, "and I will release this worthless wizard."

"Never!" cries Shaw, his hand flying to his sword. "I shall never give up the Sword of Power!"

"Then I shall never give up my new plaything!" growls the dragon, shaking the wizard like a rattle.

Shaw grabs your hand and pulls you from the room, racing back down the passageway. When you have entered the next chamber, Shaw drops your hand and says, "We must find a way to free Waldemar."

"And you won't give up your sword?" you ask.

"Never. There must be something else we can do."

"My powers are much weaker than the wizard's," you say, "but perhaps I can try to fight the dragon myself."

"I don't know," says Shaw. "That monster is thoroughly evil and has powers of magic itself."

"We seem to have no alternative," you point out, opening your spell book. "My experience in casting spells is limited, but there are a few I can try."

"What do you have in mind?" Shaw urges.

Snapping the book closed, you say, "We can either put the dragon to sleep or blind it with a fireball."

If you want to cast a Sleep Spell,
turn to page 128.

But if you think it would be safer to blind it
with a Fireball Spell, turn to page 101.

"Let's go through Blissford," you say. "It may be a while before Ungaar thinks to search for me there."

"Blissford it is, along the Castle River," says Shaw, unclasping the flap of his knapsack. "I'll put the scroll and the map in here, and we're on our way."

You hold tightly to your valuables, not sure that you care to be so trusting just yet.

"Go ahead, Mialie," urges Worm. "The prince isn't going to steal them." She swoops down to your shoulder, whispering, "The only treasure he might steal is your heart. That's what you'll have to watch out for."

"Hush, Worm!" you hiss. You glance toward Shaw to see if he's listening, but he's busy arranging his backpack. "He's coming along as a guide and a fighter," you whisper, "and that's all, do you understand?"

But you feel yourself blushing again. You hand Shaw your map and scroll, just to silence Worm.

He places them in the pack and says, "Then we're off!"

"Good luck to you!" pipes the finch, waving you off with a golden wing.

"Thank you, Worm. Perhaps we will meet again some day," you call, hurrying along behind Shaw. You travel east, toward the rising sun, making your way through trails of mist that rise like smoke from the grasses.

"How did you get a name like 'Shaw'?" you ask, trying to make conversation.

"It means 'from the grove.' Behind Blissford Castle is a great grove of aspen, and in autumn the leaves turn golden and rustle in the wind." He smiles faintly. "My mother thought my hair looked like the autumn aspen. So she named me Shaw."

He turns to you, his fair curls bright in the morning sun. "Mialie," he says. "What a lovely name. What does it mean?"

"I wouldn't know," you say bluntly.

"Don't your parents ever talk about your name?"

You feel tension hardening your body, and your hands clench tightly the folds of your skirt. *Here he is, a prince of royal blood,* you think, *and I don't even know who I am. If I tell him the truth, he might just decide not to accompany me after all. Nonsense!* you think suddenly. *If he leaves because I'm not of noble parentage, that's his choice. I can fare perfectly well on my own.*

"I never knew who my parents were," you say, finally. "They deserted me when I was an infant."

"No," says Shaw.

"And Ungaar raised me."

"You were raised by Yorguths?" Shaw's eyes widen in disbelief. "I don't know how you survived your childhood. You certainly haven't a trace of barbarism in you."

You are pleased by his reaction and want to hear more. "So you don't think I make much of a Yorguth?" you ask. "I have red hair like they do."

"And lovely hair it is. But that's the extent of the likeness," he says flatly. "You haven't a hint of any other Yorguth trait."

"Well, then, what sorts of traits do you think I have?" you ask lightly, trying not to blush from his compliment and testing to see if he suspects your magic powers.

"Pure Gallenian strain, I would say," he states, looking you up and down objectively. "Fair coloring, inherently well-bred mannerisms, and probably sensitive and trusting deep inside."

So far so good, you think.

Then he adds, "And I detect a determination and strength that seem to stem from an inborn power."

Your jaw muscles harden. "What sort of power?" you ask, your voice strained. *He can't know I'm a sorceress, can he?* you wonder. *Does it show somehow?*

"Oh, I don't know," says Shaw. "Some people seem to have a gift that allows them to survive when others falter. I think you have that ability. Am I right?"

You breathe a sigh of relief. "Perhaps," you say. "One thing I know for certain. I'm determined to get to the cavern, now that I'm on my way."

"Then we'd better quicken our pace, before the Yorguths are after us," says Shaw. He strides ahead, moving smoothly and easily, and you hurry to keep up with him.

Soon the trees and brush disappear behind you, and you enter a great expanse of marshland, where long fingers of water cut through the sand.

"It's the river delta," says Shaw. "Now we'll head south, but be careful where you step. There's a lot of quicksand ar—"

And before the warning is out of his mouth, his long stride plunges him into mucky sand. He instantly begins to sink.

"Don't come near me!" he cries, his boots already half-buried. You leap back, away from the quicksand, and watch, horror-stricken and helpless, as he sinks deeper and deeper still.

"I must do something, Shaw!" you cry. "How can I get you out of there?"

He struggles against the quicksand, his face pale as death, his gray eyes fearful. You scan the marsh for a long stick, a log, anything to help lift him out. But there is not a tree in sight.

"Here, try to grab the end of this," he says, pointing his sword toward you.

You reach out as far as you can. "I can't!" you cry. "It's not long enough!" Panic creeps up your spine. "What if I run back for a tree branch?"

"Perhaps, Mialie," he says. "If you hurry. But I'm sinking fast."

And he is. The quicksand has sucked him down to the waist now, and he closes his eyes in surrender.

I could cast a spell, you think. *A Levitation Spell would surely save him. But then he will know the truth about my powers, and what if he tells Ungaar? What if he tells anyone at all? I would be ruined.*

Shaw is buried to his chest now. You are faced with two choices.

If you try casting a spell, turn to page 35.

If you run back to the edge of the marsh to find a branch, turn to page 60.

"Come on, Shaw, let's run!" you shout. You lean low over your horse and hug your knees tightly into its sides, yelling, "Faster, faster!" The horse gallops like wildfire, overtaking Shaw, past streams and rocks, through a mountain pass, so fast you don't dare look back. You just listen to the wind whistling past your ears and clasp the steed's mane with both hands.

Up ahead you see a tangle of brush. "Jump!" you yell, but before you know it, the horse has caught its hoof, and you are hurled through the air, landing face down on the grass. You turn over in time to see your horse scramble to its feet and take off across the valley.

"Shaw," you moan, but he is gone. You hear galloping hooves, and through the mountain pass rides Ungaar, his Yorguths storming behind. He dismounts and stalks toward you, his blue eyes bright with fury. His very presence makes you tremble.

"You have made a grave error, my child. A very grave error in judgment." His hand strokes his pointed beard, and he paces slowly, methodically, before you.

"You disappoint me. My heart is wounded, aching." He shakes his head in mock distress. "My own adopted daughter, who so humbly took the Oath of Fealty years ago, now abandoning me. How faithless you have been, my Mialie. How disobedient!"

He tightens his lips until they go white, and his blazing eyes burn through you like pokers.

"Why? Why? Is it the young man you were with? Did he force you to escape in the night?" He leans forward, his pockmarked face now just inches from yours. "This I promise you: he shall be dealt with. My army will find him and teach him where your loyalties lie.

"And as for you," he continues, drawing his sword

and running his finger along its edges. "How shall I punish you for the pain you have caused your lord?"

I don't care what you do to me, you think. *Just don't hurt Shaw. He did nothing wrong.* But you know better than to challenge Ungaar. Silence is the only way to cool his hot temper, and you lower your eyes, not saying a word.

His black boots are circling you, around and around, as if he is pondering your punishment.

"This time," he says finally, "this time I shall be compassionate. But only this once. Should there be another incident of disobedience, my rage will know no mercy. Do you understand?" He points the sword at your throat.

"You shall spend a fortnight in the Lost Abbey, where the clerics shall see that you fast and repent for your faithless act. They shall be under my strictest orders. Now get down on your knees and apologize to your lord."

Your anger at this humiliation pounds through your veins, but you are silent, and you kneel before him as he places his sword on your head.

"I am sorry, Lord and Master Ungaar," you mumble.

"Louder!" he commands. "My men can't hear you."

"I am sorry!" you shout, hoping that Shaw is nowhere nearby to see you subject yourself to such treatment.

A cruel smirk spreads across Ungaar's face, and he replaces his sword in its sheath.

"To the abbey!" he cries to his men, who come forward to lift you up on horseback.

They carry you far into the valley and down a hidden trail that leads deep into a dark hollow, protected on all sides by hills. Nestled within is the abbey, a mighty structure of gray stone. You hear a bell tolling as you pass through the iron gates. A hooded cleric meets you at the entrance.

"She is to remain solitary for a fortnight," growls Ungaar. "No food, no visitors." The cleric nods without murmuring a word. She must fear Ungaar, too, you think. She accepted his command unflinchingly. She leads you away, past huge gargoyles, beneath marble arches, down an ancient passageway, into a cell.

You have heard of these clerics, women who spend their days in meditation, taking in the sick and the unfortunate, nursing them back to health. You wonder how they have survived the onslaught of the barbarian

Yorguths, these quiet clerics with their peaceful ways.

You are alone now in the cell, staring at the rusty drops of water oozing down the stone walls. You can hear some sort of ritual beginning, and you cross to the window to watch.

Down below, a procession of hooded clerics crosses the courtyard, chanting an ancient hymn. The music is comforting, but the language is foreign to you, and you open your spell book to find a way to understand the words.

Suddenly, you hear a key rattling in the door lock, and you slip down to the floor, hiding your book beneath your skirt. The door creaks open, and a very old cleric enters, her leathered face shadowed by her hood.

"I'm glad you've come," she whispers. "I always knew we would meet one day."

What does she mean? you wonder. But you keep quiet, waiting to see if she will explain herself. You see that her apron is brimming with wild flowers, and she carries a basket of food in her arms.

"I've brought you dark bread with rosemary honey, and I've put a drop of wine in your water, for flavor," she tells you.

"That's very kind of you," you say. "But I thought Lord Ungaar ordered me to fast."

"My dear," she answers, "we do not run a prison here. You are a young girl, and must have energy. Now, come. Take the basket and eat."

As you stand up, your black book tumbles to the floor. You quickly snatch it up and put it in your pocket.

The old cleric has seen it, and her eyes narrow as

she gently asks,. "Is that your spell book, my dear?"

Your heart freezes.

"It's just a private journal," you say. "Nothing very interesting."

"A private journal of your magic spells, you mean," says the cleric, slyly. "Your parents were magic-users, you know, and the powers are passed from generation to generation. Oh, not to worry," she says, setting the basket down on the floor. "I won't tell Ungaar."

"But how do you know about my magic, about my parents, about . . ." Your mind is bombarded with questions, and you want to ask them all at once.

"I was there, my dear," says the cleric, hobbling toward the door. "Now eat your food."

"You were where?" you cry, rushing to clutch her arm. "Wait! Don't leave. I want to know . . . who were they? Who were my parents?"

"All in due time," whispers the cleric, a smile creeping across her withered face. "You shall be here for a while, and I will visit every day. By the time you leave, we shall know each other well, my dear. Very well." She turns when she reaches the door. "And keep practicing with your book. Someday you will understand your gift, and you will use it wisely."

She disappears and you slide slowly down the wall, bewildered. You reach for a chunk of bread and nibble on it absently, falling into daydreams of your parents and the scroll and Shaw. Before you know it, your cell has darkened with the night.

You suddenly realize that you hear soft music floating in through the window. It is not the solemn chanting of the clerics, but a light, soothing song played on a stringed instrument, and you creep to the window

to look outside.

Down below is Shaw, his blond curls white in the moonlight. Strumming his mandolin, he smiles up at you. Your heart beats wildly with joy and disbelief.

"What are you . . ." you begin, but he raises a finger to his lips to silence you. He pulls a rope from his belt and tosses it up. Once you have fastened it around the stone sill, he climbs up and jumps through the window, his eyes glistening.

"Well, aren't you pleased to see me?" he asks.

Pleased, yes. But I won't give him the satisfaction of a compliment, you think. "I was doing quite well on my own," you say. "You needn't have gone out of your way."

He lights up this room like a star, you think, as he settles into a corner with his mandolin. *Perhaps I should let him know how pleased I am to see him, after all. But no,* you think, *I'm not ready for that yet. If we start to talk about our feelings, I'll have to tell him the truth about my sorcery.*

Your heart is gripped with fear just at the thought. *He's along only as my guide,* you say to yourself. *And I intend to keep my distance.* You stare out the window in silence.

"I wrote a song for you, Mialie. Would you like to hear it?"

Your heart leaps. A song. Just for you. But you control your feelings and glance at him coolly. "What, and wake the entire abbey so they lock you up, too? No, not now," you say, dying to hear the words.

"Then come with me into the valley, and I'll sing it for you," he says brightly.

"If I leave, and Ungaar finds me a second time,

there will be no mercy. He'll imprison me forever, Shaw."

"And if you stay? You'll go back and be imprisoned in the fields. Come, Mialie. If we leave now, while the clerics are sleeping, we can make the cavern by tomorrow night."

If I go with him, you think, *I may never find out who my parents were, and I may never see the old cleric again.* Shaw is standing at the window waiting for you, his mandolin slung over his shoulder.

If you think you should stay at the abbey and hope to escape sometime in the future, turn to page 47.

If you want to escape with Prince Shaw, turn to page 98.

"Let's take the quickest route," you say, rolling up the map. "The Caves of Gallendale."

"The caves it is!" agrees the prince. "I've battled goblins before and can do it again. And I have a torch to help light our way," he adds, patting his knapsack.

"Caves!" mumbles Worm, shuddering so her feathers fluff her up into a golden ball. "Not a good place for birds. Too dark and dreary."

She flies to your shoulder then, whispering, "But I'm sure you'll be fine, Mialie. Shaw can protect your head and you just protect your heart. I've heard, these handsome princes can be deadly heartbreakers."

"Enough, Worm!" you hiss, hoping that Shaw didn't hear her chattering. "Thank you for your help. Perhaps our paths will cross again some day."

The finch flies off in the morning fog, and you hand the scroll and the map to Shaw. "Why don't you keep them in your knapsack for now?" you say.

"You mean you trust me that much already?" he asks, smiling, and you instantly regret your decision. You reach toward the knapsack to snatch them back, but his hand is faster than yours, and he has locked the clasp.

"Don't worry, Mialie," he says, his eyes bright. "I'm a most trustworthy person. Your valuables will be safe with me, I assure you."

You believe him, for some reason. There seems to be an aura of honesty about him that you have never found in the Yorguths.

"It's a long journey to the cave entrance," Shaw is saying. He is heading for the rocky hills in the distance, his long stride taking him ahead of you. "Perhaps I should strum a song or two on the way."

You are practically running, trying to keep up with him. "Not a good idea," you say, puffing. "It might attract attention."

"Then I suppose we could spend the time getting to know each other." He glances back over his shoulder at you. "Mialie . . . What a lovely name. Is that a family name?"

You set your jaw hard, feeling tension hardening your muscles. "I wouldn't know," you say.

"Don't your parents ever talk about your name?" he asks, ignoring the coldness in your voice.

"No," you say, trying to think of a way to change the subject. *If he knew the truth, he'd probably turn around and head back the way he came,* you tell yourself.

You watch him, his stride long and easy, a smooth elegance in his movements. *A prince can be comfortable with anyone,* you think. *His noble status makes him welcome anywhere. But an abandoned orphan is uneasy with every person she meets—uncomfortable with the Yorguths, with royalty, even with herself.* Your stomach is a hard, tense knot now.

"They say those who talk little think a great deal," says Shaw. "Just what thoughts are running through your head right now, Mialie?" His tone is light, casual.

This silk-robed prince with the carefree smile has the right to be casual about life, you think, *but as for me . . .*

Suddenly, you straighten up, tossing your auburn hair indignantly. *Why should I care what he thinks of me, anyway? I barely even know him . . .*

"I don't have any parents, Prince Shaw," you say

boldly. "They deserted me when I was an infant." *There,* you think, *it's out.*

Shaw stops to turn and look at you, his eyes shadowed by a frown. "How awful for you, Mialie," he says. "And if they only knew what a beautiful young woman you would turn out to be. What a strong, beautiful woman."

His reaction takes you by surprise. You stare at him in disbelief and immediately shift your gaze to the ground, not knowing what to say.

"I grew up without parents, too," he continues. "They were executed by the Yorguths when I was five." You look up at him now, and his eyes are cloudy. "I was raised by the clerics at Blissford Abbey, until I went off on my own two years ago," he says.

"I think we have a lot in common, Mialie," he says. "I feel very strongly about that. I felt it the moment I met you."

You want to tell him how you feel, too. You want to tell him that he is different, and trustworthy, and much more attractive than any Yorguth you've known, but instead, you look off toward the hills.

"The sun is burning the fog off the ground now," you say. "We'd best hurry along."

Shaw sighs and walks along beside you. Your strides match now, yours a little longer and bolder than before, his slower, his enthusiasm dampened somewhat.

Please turn to page 50.

WHOOSH! A dagger has whizzed through the air just an inch from Shaw's head and pierced the trunk of an oak tree. You both drop to the ground.

Your eyes scan the area, but you can see nothing lurking in the surrounding woods. Glancing up at the tree, you can see a small piece of bark dangling from the dagger.

"It looks as if the coast is clear," says Shaw. "Let's take a look at this knife."

He moves cautiously toward the oak tree and pulls out the dagger.

"These are some very strange scribblings," he says, examining the piece of bark. "Can you make anything out of this?"

You take the bark from his hand, inspecting the script. "It's elven," you say. "I'm certain it's written in elven."

"It probably says 'No Trespassing' or 'Keep Out—Elven Territory,' " says Shaw.

"No," you say, reading the message slowly. "It reads 'Come see me, Young Fighter. I have wonders to show you.' "

"What does that mean?" asks Shaw.

"I've no idea," you answer, searching the woods for a sign of elves. "I think we'd best ignore it."

But as you speak, you see that Shaw's eyes are alight with curiosity, and he moves to an enormous oak tree across from the dagger. There is an open doorway in the hollow trunk, and a wooden ladder wound with morning glories leans against the tree's dark interior. Outside the tree high up toward the branches, a window has been cut, complete with tiny shutters and a flower-filled box.

"This must be the place," says Shaw, his eyes bright. "I think we should check this out."

"You're just asking for trouble, Shaw," you warn, perturbed. "And besides, if we keep getting distracted this way, we'll never get to the cavern." But your words fall on deaf ears. His curiosity tempts him, and he is already ducking through the doorway.

"Are you coming, Mialie?" he asks.

"No, Shaw," you say sadly. "I'll go on to the cavern alone while you explore the tree."
Turn to page 45.

"Yes, Shaw, if that's what you want."
Turn to page 113.

I think Bethany would look charming with a mustache, you decide, looking at her dancing eyes and her white teeth and her bare shoulders. You stare at her, concentrating, and soon there is a dark shadow on her upper lip. It grows darker and darker, until a waxy black mustache has bloomed on her dainty face.

You lean back in your chair and smile faintly.

Suddenly, a girl at Bethany's table jumps to her feet, screaming, "Bethany! What's happened to you? You have . . . you have . . . a mustache, Bethany!"

Heads turn from all directions, and soon all eyes are on Bethany.

"That's ridiculous!" she snaps. But she moves her fingers across her lips, and suddenly her eyes widen and she leaps up crying, "How could this be? I've never in my life . . ." And off she flies, black curls jiggling, to find a place to hide.

Slowly, very slowly, Shaw turns to you. You sit, cool and composed, just ready to bite into a chunk of bread, when his hand grabs your wrist and his face moves just inches from yours.

"It was you, wasn't it, Mialie?" he demands. "You made Bethany grow a mustache, didn't you? Well, didn't you?"

The harshness of his tone makes you tremble, and you drop the bread onto your plate and lower your eyes.

"Tell me the truth, Mialie."

"Yes," you say quietly. "I did it."

"How can you use your powers in such an irresponsible manner?" he bursts out. "Use them for your own pleasure? I can't believe . . ."

Before he can finish, you are up and out the door,

racing as fast as you can from the inn, from Bethany, from Shaw. Shame fills your heart and drives you faster and faster into the darkness. Soon you find yourself in a tangle of vines on the outskirts of the woods. You try to rip the vines from your legs and arms, but the more you try, the more entangled you become. You fling yourself to the ground, sobbing, ashamed of yourself.

I've behaved disgracefully, you think. *I don't deserve the gift I have. I belittled my magic powers in order to fulfill a whim.*

Suddenly, you feel a hand stroking your hair. You raise your head to see Shaw, his eyes no longer dark with anger, but gentle and soft.

"Mialie," he says quietly. "It's not the end of the world."

You shake your head violently, trying to free yourself from his touch.

"Leave me alone, Shaw," you cry. "Just take your mandolin and your jokes and head back to the inn. I assure you, Bethany's mustache is gone now. The two of you can have a good laugh at my irresponsible behavior. Go on!"

Shaw does not take his hands from you. He cups your face between them and looks gently into your eyes.

"I don't want to go back to the inn, Mialie. I want to stay here with you."

"Why on earth would you want to do that, Shaw? After I've made such a fool . . ."

"Don't you know that you are very special to me?" he asks.

Your eyes widen, but you are silent.

"Mialie, let me tell you something. Bethany knows I'm a prince, and she's impressed with my title, not with me. You're different, Mialie. With you, I'm real. And that's important to me."

"It's important to me, too, Shaw," you say. "I could never be myself with the Yorguths, always hiding my magic powers from them, always feeling like an outcast. I've never been more real with anyone before. Not ever."

Shaw leans toward you then and brushes your lips with his, lightly, gently. You feel a glow rush through your body, and you sigh softly, feeling the warmth of his breath on your cheek.

"We'll get to the cavern, Mialie," he says. "And we'll do it together."

He pulls you to your feet and clasps your hand tightly, leading you out of the vines and along the riverbank.

Please turn to page 65.

You pull your spell book from your pocket, whipping through the pages to find a Levitation Spell.

I have no time to lose worrying about what the prince will say, you tell yourself. *His life is at stake.*

The magic words spill from your lips, and you raise your arms toward Shaw. FLASH! Green sparks fly from your fingers, surrounding him. Instantly, he floats from the quicksand, landing muddy and drenched on the marsh grass beside you.

He opens his eyes wide in astonishment.

"I can't believe it!" he cries. "You're a wizard, Mialie! A powerful, magical wizard!"

For a moment, you think he's going to hug you, muddy clothes and all, and you take a step backward, catching your breath.

"Well, I wouldn't exactly say that . . ." you mumble, feeling confused and afraid and wonderfully powerful, all at the same time.

"You saved my life!" cries Shaw, still so amazed that he hasn't bothered to brush the wet sand from his garments. "I was shoulder-deep in that . . ."

He stops abruptly, the wonderment in his eyes darkening to fear. "Do you hear that?" he whispers.

Far in the distance, the thunder of horses' hooves rapidly increases in intensity. Wild war cries pierce the foggy air, sending a chill through your heart.

"It's the Yorguths!" you cry. "Hurry, we have no time to waste!"

You race along the river, the blood beating rapidly through your veins. Even in your panic, you are careful not to step too close to the river, where the sand is mucky and wet.

"There's an old tower up ahead!" Shaw says, panting. "The Tower of Desolation. It's half-crumbling and gloomy but a decent place to hide."

"Lead on," you say.

The bellows of the barbarians carry down the river as you speed ahead. You envision them storming across the tall grasses toward you, his blazing eyes searching you out. *His fits of rage are so unpredictable!* you think. *If he captures me, he may even execute me on the spot.*

"They're getting louder and closer!" you cry.

"Keep up your pace, Mialie!" shouts Shaw. "The tower is on the bluff up ahead!"

You race straight for the bluff and begin to climb, breathless from the exertion. The underbrush is thick and thorny, and you lift up your skirt to keep it from getting caught. *The horses will never get through this tangled brush,* you think. *If the Yorguths come this way, they'll have to dismount.*

You follow Shaw into the woods, along an overgrown path. Suddenly, right before you, a dilapidated tower looms taller than the trees. It is black and crumbling, with a great wooden door facing the river.

Shaw lunges toward the door, throwing the weight of his body against it. The door crashes open and you rush inside.

Dank odors fill your nostrils, and your face is instantly entwined in cobwebs, but you slam the door behind you, feeling safe and out of sight.

"Quick, Mialie! Up the staircase!"

Shaw takes the stone steps two at a time. You scramble up behind him in the darkness. Soon you are in a clammy stone chamber at the very top of the tower.

Shaw crosses to the one tiny window in the room.

"They're riding to the west, skirting the woods," he announces. "They didn't see us come this way."

"Thank goodness," you say, sighing. "We can stay here for a while and leave when they're a safe distance away."

"Exactly," says Shaw. Then he turns to you, his eyes brightening. "So how does milady fancy the accommodations?"

"If the spiders moved out, I'd be more comfortable," you say, pulling silky webs from your eyes and hair and brushing the spiders off your blouse.

"Well, cast a spell and get rid of them," he says with a grin.

You shoot him an annoyed look and continue picking the bugs off your clothes.

"I'm sorry," he says. "I didn't mean to make fun of your wizardry."

"Would you stop calling it that, please?" you snap.

"Well, what would you call it then?" he asks.

You dislodge a tiny spider from your hair and watch it scurry off across the floor. "Ungaar would call it witchcraft," you say, "evil and wicked."

Shaw doesn't respond right away. He slides down to the floor and slips his mandolin from his shoulder. After knocking some dried mud from its base, he begins strumming it softly.

You watch him, his fair curls bent over the mandolin, his long fingers gentle. *He is easy and elegant even in his muddy garments, even in this dreary, dark setting. It's as if he carries the sunlight inside him.*

He looks up at you, his gaze direct. "Don't talk like a Yorguth, Mialie,"he says suddenly.

"I'm not talking like a Yorguth," you say, taken

aback. "I'm telling you how I feel about my powers."

A shadow crosses his gray eyes. He stops strumming and leans on the mandolin. "Then I'm sorry for your feelings, Mialie," he says quietly. "Because if you think saving my life was an evil act, driven by wicked powers of sorcery, then I don't know what to tell you."

You stare down at the dusty floor in silence. *Shaw is right,* you think. *How could my power be evil if I would never use it in a vengeful or cruel manner?* The thought of a magic-user being good never occurred to you before. It's almost too much to believe.

"Aren't you just a bit afraid to think that I levitated you from that quicksand, Shaw?"

"Not at all. I thought you were wonderful, splendid, stupendous." He grins, his eyes crinkling at the edges. "And I would never say those things to a wicked witch, believe me."

You smile in spite of yourself. "But if Ungaar ever discovered me, I'd be executed in a minute."

"No need to worry about Ungaar now," says Shaw. "Come and sit by me. I'll play a song for you."

He reaches his hand toward you, but you back off slightly. *Why am I afraid for him to touch me?* you muse. *He's so warm and kind.* But you are afraid—afraid of Worm's ridiculous warning. You don't trust the melting feeling that glows inside when you watch him from the corner of your eye.

I will not let these feelings interfere with my journey, you decide. *He's with me to fight off enemies we might encounter and to guide me down the river, and that's all.*

You turn away from Shaw and look out the window. "What kind of song?" you ask, ignoring his hand.

"Never mind," he says, his voice quiet with disappointment. "You wouldn't want to hear it anyway." He strums softly for a while, and you feel an uncomfortable silence building between you. You push the feeling to the back of your mind and think about your powers instead. "Trust your powers rare,' the scroll had read. *And without even realizing it,* you think, *I have chosen good. I may indeed be a sorceress of good powers.*

For the first time in your life, you feel comfortable to have your spell book in your pocket.

"Well, shall we be on our way?" Shaw asks. "The Yorguths should be far down the river by now."

His voice startles you. You had been completely lost in thoughts of magic.

"Yes," you say. "That's a good idea."

Shaw opens the door that leads to the stairway. Before you know what's happening, he slams it shut again and leaps back to the center of the tower chamber, his hand flying to his sword.

Please turn to page 54.

"Let's go through the valley," you say. "We'll just steer clear of town."

"You'd best be on your way," says Worm, looking at the sky, pale from the dawn. "Good luck to you both."

She gives you a peck on the cheek and flies over to Shaw. When he kisses her outstretched wing, she glances over at you, rolling her eyes, as if she's going to swoon.

You scowl at her in irritation, and turn away. "Good-bye, Worm," you say firmly. "Thank you for all your help."

Off flies the finch, disappearing in the blue fog. You and Shaw head toward the valley. In the distance, you can hear the neighing of horses. Soon you can see galloping toward you two wild white horses speckled with gray, their manes whipping in the wind.

"We'll ride them," says Shaw. "It will be much faster than traveling on foot. Do you know how to ride, Mialie?"

"Of course," you answer, pleased that you can demonstrate one of your skills.

"Okay," says Shaw. "They're slowing down now. Get ready to run beside the horse on the right, grab his mane, and mount him."

Before you know it, the horse is right beside you, and he looks enormous, frightening. Your heart pounds as you race alongside, reaching to grasp the mane in your hands. The steed does not halt, and you cling to his neck, scrambling to get your leg over his back. At last you are firmly planted atop the horse, and off you fly across the valley.

Shaw is galloping by your side. You see that he is a fine equestrian, riding tall and princely, his jeweled sword at his side. He smiles at you, and you turn away, embarrassed that you were watching him.

Suddenly, far behind you, you hear wild warlike cries and the drumming of hooves. "It looks like the girl!" you hear someone shout. You turn to see several Yorguths charging, their wooden shields in hand. They are armed with axes, ready for battle.

"It's Ungaar's army!" you cry. "They've spotted me!"

"Do you think we can outrun them?" shouts Shaw.

"I don't know. They're master horsemen."

Your steed speeds ahead, and you glance back to see that the Yorguths are not yet gaining on you.

"There's a shelter in the mountainside ahead where we can hide," says Shaw. "Should we stop?"

Your mind is racing in a fearful panic, the howls of the Yorguths bringing back a rush of memories. You've seen them torture with relish those they considered disloyal. *And now,* you think, *I am disloyal myself, running away in the night. If they catch me, they will be merciless.*

"We have to make up our minds now, Mialie!" shouts Shaw. "What do you want to do?"

If you think you can outrun the Yorguths, turn to page 19.

But if you would rather hide in the mountain shelter, turn to page 58.

You push your chair back from the table and stalk out of the inn without even saying good-bye. You race down the cobblestone street, out across the fields toward the bluff.

I don't need him, you think. *I would have been better off on my own from the beginning! And as for that giggling girl . . .*

"Mialie!" you hear. "Mialie, wait!"

I'm not going to stop and turn around for him, you think. *I wouldn't give him the satisfaction.*

You race ahead, but soon Shaw catches up with you, and he runs at your side.

"Stop, Mialie!" he says. "Stop for just a minute!"

You stop abruptly and turn to glare at him. "What is it that you want, Shaw of Blissford?" you demand.

Slowly, a grin spreads across his face, crinkling his eyes at the edges.

"Why, I do believe your eyes are green, Mialie," he teases. "Greener than I've ever seen them."

"Why don't you march right back into the inn and tell Bethany another funny story?" you fume. "I'm sure she'll laugh her pretty little head off!"

"Bethany is the friendly type, isn't she?" His eyes are dancing with amusement. "She doesn't back away when I touch her, did you notice?"

"I noticed." You scowl, refusing to yield to his charm. "And I really don't care if you stay. I have more important things to do than sit and flirt all evening."

You spin around on your heel to walk away, and Shaw grabs your waist from behind. You squirm, trying to get away, but he holds you firmly.

"Turn around and fight your battle," he says, not letting go of you. "And magic won't work this time.

This time we're talking about matters of the heart."

You turn to face him and find that the amusement has left his eyes. He is more serious than you have ever seen him.

"You're different, Mialie," he says suddenly. "Not like all the Bethanys of the world. Bethany knows I'm a prince, even if my family no longer rules. My title impresses her, not me. With you . . . with you I feel real."

He takes his hands from your waist and cups your face with them gently. "You're special, Mialie, really special."

Your heart glows. Suddenly, you feel an aura settling in around the two of you, a golden aura of happiness and warmth and protection. You raise your head and smile into his eyes.

"We have a mission to complete," he says. "And I wouldn't miss it for the world. Let's go."

He takes your hand in his, and you head off along the riverbank.

Please turn to page 65.

You sigh in exasperation. "I can't be led off track, Shaw!" you moan. I feel that something important is waiting for me at the cavern. I'm going on ahead. Are you coming with me?"

He doesn't even answer you. It's as if he's in a trance, climbing up the wooden ladder to the tree.

I need to make up for lost time! you think. *Now that I don't have to worry that Shaw will see me use my powers, I'll cast a spell that will make me fly. It'll get me at least a short distance.*

You search the ground for a bird feather, and open your book to the spell. With a few magic words, and the feather in your hand, you soar into the air and head through the valley. But a rising fog obscures your vision, and soon you find you are very lost, engulfed in thick white clouds.

As the spell ends, you descend until you land beside a winding river. *I wonder how far I am from the cavern now?* you think, your heart sinking. *If only I had the map with me!*

You see that night is falling, and you lean against a tree, trying to decide what to do. Suddenly, a figure appears in the foggy mist, a man walking along the river in your direction. You can make out the color of his garments, blue, and you see a sword fastened at his side.

"Shaw!" you cry. "I can't believe you're here!"

"Mialie?" he shouts, running toward you. "I can't believe *you're* here!" He throws his arms around you, hugging you tightly. "I'm so happy to see you!"

You wrap your arms around his waist, hugging him back. I'm actually hugging him, you say to yourself. And you feel wonderful.

"That message was from a beguiling little tree sprite!" he says. "She took me over here by the river, as far away from you as she thought she could, and nearly charmed me. But I kept thinking of you, Mialie, and how I promised to help you get to the cavern, and I finally had the strength to run from her, and here I am! And here you are!" he cries, still not able to believe it. "I'm so glad to be with you again!"

"Me, too," you say, feeling very good to say what you think, no longer hiding your feelings. "But it's nearly nightfall, and I have no idea where to go from here. Do you still have the map?"

"We don't need it," says Shaw. "We're in my homeland now. Come on, just follow me."

He takes your hand and leads you along the riverbank.

Please turn to page 65.

"It is best that I stay and obey my orders," you say, not looking at Shaw. "I know it is best."

"If that is your decision, Mialie," he says quietly, "then I will respect it."

"But sometime I would like to hear your song," you say. "I really would, Shaw."

"Well, I should be off now," he says, playing with the strings of his mandolin, as if he is stalling for time. Then he nods and climbs slowly out the window to the ground, leaving his rope hanging from the stone sill.

You fall into a sleep full of tangled dreams, of people fading away before you can make them stay.

In the morning, the old cleric shuffles through the doorway with more bread and a huge red pear.

"Did you sleep well, my dear?" she asks.

"No," you say. "I dreamed of my parents. I really must know more," you say intently, grasping her arm. "Please tell me more."

The cleric looks at you, her old eyes narrowing. Then she limps over to the door and shuts it carefully.

"Your parents were very important people, Mialie," she says, watching your reaction closely.

"Sorcerers, weren't they?" you ask. "My parents were some kind of evil sorcerers . . ."

"Evil?" cries the old cleric. "Heavens, no! You see, my dear, there are magic-users of all shapes and sizes, all mentalities and persuasions. It just so happens that your parents were very fine and very good, the best kind of magic-users." She moves close to you, her hood touching your face, and you feel as if you are peering into a cave. "Have you figured out who your parents were?"

"No," you say. "I haven't. I really don't know."

"The King and Queen of Gallendale," she says triumphantly. "And you, my dear, are the Princess of Gallendale."

"No!" you say, barely a whisper escaping. "That can't be. I'm . . ."

"You are very special," she says, "with wonderful powers of magic. Your parents always used theirs in the best possible way."

"But that means Ungaar stole me from my parents. He never found me in the marsh . . ."

From outside the window comes a growling voice: "Now I've got you, Mialie. Trying to escape, eh?"

The hulking form of Buchfric, a Yorguth warrior who who always disliked you, appears in the window. He jumps inside, tense as an animal that has cornered its prey. From his hand trails the end of Shaw's rope.

"It is most unfortunate that you have chosen to disobey Ungaar a second time," he says, panting from his climb up the rope. "And now that you have, you will spend the rest of your days in prison! Here is the proof!" he sneers, dangling the rope before you.

"No! You don't understand. The rope. . ." You end your protest in midsentence. You don't want to get Shaw involved. *Ungaar might punish me,* you think, *but he would surely kill Shaw.*

"Your punishment will be far worse than a fortnight at this abbey," Buchfric is saying. "Your 'caretakers' will be far less concerned with your comforts than these spineless sisters of mercy."

The cleric retreats to the corner of the cell while Buchfric ties you up. Then he throws you over his shoulder and lumbers out of the cell. You glance back at the cleric, huddled in the corner, her face old and sad in the shadow of her hood. But you detect a faint smile, and she nods to you.

Somehow, you think, *somehow I will find a way to defeat Ungaar. After all, I still have my spell book, and I am a princess, the Princess of Gallendale!*

But right now, as you hang like a slaughtered lamb over Buchfric's shoulder, you aren't sure just how you'll do it. You realize that, for the time being, you have come to . . .

THE END

After hiking for some time, you reach the Caves of Gallendale. Outside the light falls on the brush, and the stones are sun-bleached and warm to the touch. But as soon as you pass through the rocky mouth of the cave, all is dark. You shudder, feeling that this darkness holds unpleasant and violent secrets.

Shaw lights his torch immediately. It flickers eerily, casting long, curving shadows on the cave walls.

"We're not taking any chances in here," he says. "It's so easy to take the wrong passage. With a light we can at least minimize the surprises."

And surprises there will be, you think, *in this ancient stillness where stalactites jut from the roof like stony icicles.* You must thread your way through their counterparts, stalagmites, thrusting up from the floor. *I feel like I'm in a tomb,* you think.

"Worm was right," you say. "She would have hated it in here, without even a peephole to see the sky."

Shaw is too busy organizing to respond. "We need to leave markers, Mialie, so we can return to the entrance if we get lost. Here, hold this for a minute," he says, handing you the torch. He rummages through his knapsack, looking for markers. "Nothing. I haven't a thing to use."

"What about strips of fabric?" you offer. "I have plenty of material in the hem of my skirt."

"Perfect," says Shaw, as you tear tiny bits off the edge of your skirt. *I hope the passage isn't too long,* you think, *or I might not have a skirt left when we reach the end.*

You travel the maze of passageways far into the depths of the cave, dropping your markers every few feet. Soon you pass through a narrow tunnel that opens into a huge, echoing chamber. Bats flap their wings loudly, diving overhead. You move from wall to wall, Shaw shining the torchlight in every crevice, searching for a way out.

"There's got to be a way out of here somewhere," he says. But behind every crevice is a solid wall of rock, and there is no exit from the huge empty chamber.

"No!" you moan. "Is this a dead end?"

"It looks that way," says Shaw, shaking his head. "Here, let's take a look at the map." You open his pack and take out the map. Together, you lean toward it and study the route carefully.

"It looks as though we took the wrong passageway back near the entrance," says Shaw. "This part of the cave isn't even on the map."

You are suddenly very weary, and you're irritated that you hadn't consulted the map in the first place. You stuff the map back into the knapsack.

"Let's head back out," you say, as you begin retracing your steps along the markers.

Soon you are standing in a great, dank chamber. Coppery water drips from rocky cracks, and enormous stalactites and stalagmites loom like monsters all about.

"I don't remember this chamber . . . I'm sure we've never been here before, Shaw," you say, feeling the color drain from your cheeks. "Could it be that. . ." But you don't want to say it. You don't want to say the word 'lost.'

Shaw runs one hand through his curls, frowning. "This is very strange," he murmurs. "We followed the markers exactly."

You stand perfectly still, afraid to voice what you are thinking. "Someone moved the markers, didn't they?" you say at last, speaking quietly.

"It looks that way, Mialie," he answers.

"There's another passageway over there, Shaw," you whisper.

"So there is," he says, crossing to a small opening at the far end of the chamber. He pokes his head through the hole, examining it. "Whew!" he cries, pulling his head out quickly. "There's a nasty odor in there. And it sure looks like a tight squeeze. I'm not sure we can even fit through there."

You must decide which way to go from here, and you have two choices:

Continue to follow the markers.
If this is your choice, turn to page 92.

Try to squeeze through the small passageway.
Turn to page 56.

"Do you really think we'll be safe here, Shaw?" you ask.

"Yes, Mialie, I do."

"Then I shall stay with you, Shaw of Blissford. We shall live quietly and simply, free from Ungaar and his cruel Yorguths. I will use my magic to mend the tables and curtains and make this castle livable."

Having reached your decision, you now spend your days gardening and working, and in the evening Shaw plays his mandolin by the fire. Sometimes your mind is filled with questions. You think of the scroll and the cavern, you wonder about your past, your parents. But in spite of the questions, you are content. You and Shaw live peacefully day to day, hoping the Yorguths never detect your presence, hoping you are never subjected to their barbarian ways again.

THE END

Before Shaw can speak, a thunderous roar echoes down the staircase. It shakes and rattles the chamber door, vibrating through the floor and up your spine.

"What great beast has such a terrible roar?" you whisper, trembling.

"It was so dark!" says Shaw, the sword in his hand shaking. "I only saw fangs and a flash of yellow eyes, blazing eyes . . ."

You slowly back up against the wall, your eyes glued to the door. It's rattling wildly now, and you hear claws tearing away at the wood. A piercing howl screeches through the chamber again, a howl with the deep and mighty resonance of a lion's roar.

"It c-could wake the dead," you stammer.

You look at Shaw and see that he has gone pale as a ghost. Knowing you must do something, you race across to the window, hoping for an idea.

"Shaw!" you cry. "Do you have a rope?"

"It's in my knapsack," he says. He drops his sword to the floor and backs up to the window.

Tearing open the knapsack, he pulls out a rope and says, "But I know it's too short. We'd have to jump."

Leaning out the window, the rope in your hand, you see it is only half the length you need.

"Yes, it's a terrible jump," you say.

"Maybe a spell, Mia—" Shaw begins, but the words are drowned out as the beast lets out another thunderous roar, which rumbles behind the door.

The beast's claws rip right through the door and suddenly, the monster's head plunges through the jagged hole. Its jaws are thrust open in a roar of thunder, its fangs long and treacherous as sharpened blades.

"It's a lion! A lion dragon!" you scream.

"A dragonne, Mialie!" shouts Shaw, "dreaded for its horrible roar! Can you cast a spell—some kind of spell that will destroy it before it destroys us?"

"But the beast may have magical powers!" you cry. "Mine may not be strong enough to conquer it!"

"We've no time!" yells Shaw. "We must act!"

The dragonne throws back its great lion's head and bellows, the roar causing your very bones to tremble. You must act before the roaring paralyzes you.

If you think you can cast a spell,
turn to page 82.

If you want to take a chance on going
through the window and jumping from the rope,
turn to page 115.

"I hope we make it through that tiny opening," you say, watching Shaw's head disappear into the hole. He wriggles through like a snake, and you hear his voice echo from a chamber on the other side.

"Ugly territory, Mialie," he calls. "But it looks like we haven't much of a choice. Come on through!"

You squirm through the hole and poke your head out the other side. The terrain is rough and wet, with deep cracks splitting the rocky floor. A muddy stream zigzags around big boulders, and you hold your breath as long as you can to avoid breathing in the dank, nasty air.

"I don't like it in here," you whisper.

"I don't either," says Shaw. "It looks like goblin territ—"

And even before he can finish, they are everywhere—goblins. Ugly goblins with yellow eyes jump from the cracks, appear from behind rocks, and splash through the water. They wield rusty swords, crashing them against the rocks.

You race back toward the opening, scrambling as fast as you can. But before you are out, you feel a hairy hand grabbing your ankle, and with a rough jerk, you are wrenched back into the goblin-filled chamber.

"Get your filthy hands off me!" you scream, knowing as you do that it will do no good to talk to the goblins at all. They know no reason.

Now four goblins surround you, poking you with their swords, reveling in their moment of dominance.

"Good red-haired slave!" grunts one, baring his fangs at you.

You begin to kick and scream, crying, "Shaw!" But then you see that Shaw himself is pinned down by seven of the creatures and is just as helpless as you are.

With howls and chuckles, the goblins lift Shaw up over their heads. Suddenly, Shaw wrenches free of their grip, flailing his sword wildly, knocking swords and spears from goblin hands. Two of the creatures hit the floor, lying bloody and immobile.

"Smash the slave girl!" growls a goblin. "Crush her red head!"

"Don't touch her!" shouts Shaw, his sword flying.

Goblins, their eyes glimmering, rush at you, and you feel their filthy hands shaking you, jerking you, and you tremble with fear.

"I'll kill you, every last one of you!" Shaw shouts. But goblins are everywhere, and now they're enraged, baring their teeth like crazed animals.

A spell would work, you think. *A Light Spell would certainly blind them so we could escape. Goblin eyes are sensitive to light. But it will be perfectly clear to Shaw that I am a sorceress if I dare cast the spell.* You close your eyes, gripped with fear, the fear of the wicked goblins and the fear of displaying the powers that you were taught were evil.

Suddenly, you are hurled against the cave wall with terrible force, and the taste of blood fills your mouth. You must make a decision quickly!

Will you cast a Light Spell and reveal your secret to Shaw? If so, turn to page 123.

Or will you keep fighting off the goblins? Turn to page 154.

"We'd better hide," you say, and Shaw nods.

"Once we get through that narrow pass up ahead," he says, "they'll never find us. We'll duck into the shelter and free the horses. The Yorguths will follow them across the valley. I know it."

You race ahead toward the pass. It has begun to rain, a soft gray rain that makes everything dreamlike and quiet. Even the bellows of the Yorguths are muted by the mist.

Soon Shaw disappears through the pass, and your horse follows, carefully making its way over the rocks. As you emerge from the other side, Shaw calls, "Here, Mialie, I'm over here."

You circle a large boulder and see that he has dismounted at the mouth of a small cave, sheltered from view by the hills. You dismount and duck inside.

"Look at the horses," Shaw whispers, as they whinny and fly off across the valley. "They're happy to run free again. I envy them."

He starts climbing the mossy rocks, moving back into the dark protection of the cave. His hair has curled like a lamb's from the rain. You follow him, your eyes pinned to his broad, wet back. You can feel your cheeks flush from watching him, and you are thankful for the darkness.

"Here's a good place," he says, stretching out on a rock. "Come and sit down, there's plenty of room."

Stepping toward the rock, you hear the galloping of hooves outside the cave, and your body stiffens.

"Which way did they go?" you hear a Yorguth growl.

"Listen!" shouts another voice. "It sounds like the horses are heading south—toward that hill!"

"There's no time to waste!" snarls a voice you recognize as Ungaar's. "Onward!" And off they gallop, their voices fading into the distance. You sigh in relief.

"They're gone," you say, settling onto the rock beside Shaw. In the dimness, you see him leaning his head against the cave wall, quite relaxed. You wish you could be as carefree as he seems to be.

"And here we are, safe and sound," he says. He turns to look at you. "Your cheeks flushed pink out there in the rain," he says. "You looked like a spring flower."

You look down at your hands held tightly in your lap. You can hear your heart pounding in the quiet of the shelter. *I must change the subject,* you think.

"Your sword is beautiful, with all its emeralds and pearls, Shaw," you say. "Where did you find it?"

"It was my father's. It's the Sword of Power for the Kingdom of Blissford."

He hears you gasp in the darkness. "Don't be too impressed, Mialie. It hasn't the power it used to. A pearl is missing from the very end of the handle, and until the pearl is replaced, the sword is powerless."

"So the Yorguths are not the lawful rulers of either of the king . . ."

Before you can finish, Shaw springs to his feet, his hand flying to his sword.

"What is it?" you cry.

"Shhh!" he whispers. "I hear something behind the rocks. Quick! Get over against that wall!"

You leap to your feet and plaster yourself against the opposite wall, clinging to the rocks.

Please turn to page 89.

"I'll be right back!" you shout over your shoulder to Shaw, as you race toward the woods.

But before you have taken ten paces, the drumming of hooves fills the morning air, and a band of Yorguths charge out of the trees. Their red hair is gnarled from the wind, their eyes blazing. At the sight of you, they begin to beat their wooden shields with their axes to signal Ungaar and the others.

"Get her!" bellows a gruff voice.

The horses bound toward you, and you spin on your heel, racing back toward Shaw. The next moment, you are flat on the ground, your head pounding from a blow.

"Get the boy!" you hear someone holler. You lift your head to see a barbarian reaching a rope toward Shaw. Shaw grasps the end and hauls himself from the quicksand.

"How you have disappointed me, my Mialie," comes a piercing voice from behind you. You recognize it immediately as Ungaar's, and you slowly turn toward him. He has dismounted and is pacing menacingly, his boots muddy and enormous.

"How dare you betray your lord and master!" he growls. "Have you no allegiance? Does your Oath of Fealty mean nothing to you?"

He glares at you, his eyes blazing with fury. "You have wounded me deeply, unbearably. You have pierced my heart with your disobedience." His voice is heavy with mock distress.

"How shall I punish you for deserting me?" he continues. "Is there a punishment short of death that is satisfactory? Perhaps not. And yet, I feel you have been led astray. You alone could not have committed such a flagrant act of betrayal."

He pulls his sword from its sheath and runs his fingers slowly across the blade. The barbarians reach Ungaar's side carrying Shaw, and they hurl him to the ground, soaked and shivering. The overlord's sword moves slowly to Shaw's throat.

"Just tell me that this boy is the cause of your disobedience, my child, and I shall be merciful. I shall take his life and spare yours."

You look at Shaw, your heart aching at the very thought that you have caused him this pain. "No," you say, your voice quavering. "I will not."

"Speak up!" snarls Ungaar. "I cannot hear you!"

"No! Never!" you cry. "He is innocent! I am the guilty one!"

"Seize her!" bellows the overlord. "Take them both to the Fortress of Doom and lock them up. They are to be plunged into the river at dawn, with great boulders tied to their ankles!"

Two barbarians grab you, strap you with leather bands, and hurl you on horseback.

Ungaar stares at you pensively for a moment and then strides to your side. "Torment throbs in my heart, my Mialie," he says dramatically. "I'm giving you one last chance. Lay the blame on the boy, and you shall be spared."

"Never!" you spit. "It is I who left, and it is I who accept the consequences of my action."

An evil smile flashes across Ungaar's face. "So be it!" he snarls. "You choose to die a martyr, then your fate is well-deserved."

"Be off!" he growls to his men, and they lead your horse south along the river, through a tangled forest.

The Fortress of Doom is a dark castle, built of great blocks of stone and surrounded by a moat. On command, the heavy bridge lowers, and the barbarians gallop beneath an iron gate into the entry chamber.

"Throw them in the dungeon!" bellows Buchfric, Ungaar's sergeant-at-arms. "Put Gorgg on guard for the night, and he will see to it that they are drowned at dawn!"

Huge Yorguth hands jerk you from the horse, and you are dragged down a stone stairway and hurled into the dungeon. The guard Gorgg rips Shaw's sword from its sheath. "You won't be needing this anymore!" he growls. The heavy door slams shut, and a key clatters in the lock.

Shaw slumps to the ground. "If it weren't for my clumsiness, falling into that quicksand, Mialie," he says, "you'd be free and on your way to the cavern."

"No use worrying about who's to blame," you say. "We must think of a way to escape."

Shaw is thoughtful for a moment and then says, "Perhaps I can attack the guard when he returns. He'll surely have a weapon with him. I could try to seize it when he enters. Our biggest problem then would be getting past the rest of the Yorguths."

"We have until dawn to decide," you say. You know your other option—your magic. *I'm not even certain I know a spell that could save us,* you think. *And besides, perhaps it's better that Shaw never knows the truth about me.*

Shaw pulls his mandolin from his shoulder and begins to strum a tune. His clear voice brightens the darkness of the dungeon, and you lean against the wall, watching him. *Even in this gloomy place, with his gar-*

ments soaked and muddy, he is easy and elegant, you think. *It's as if he carries the brightness in his heart.*

He sings about a bard who is bidding farewell to all the birds and animals as he goes to the gallows.

"Mialie," he says quietly, when the song is done. "I hope we don't have to die."

You bury your face in your hands, unable to bear the thought.

"Ever since we met," he continues, "I felt we would have time to get to know each other, time to grow."

You feel his hand touch yours, comforting you. You lean toward him, and he wraps his arms around you, holding you tightly.

It seems only minutes have passed when you hear the footsteps of the guard echo down the corridor.

"We must have dozed off!" you cry.

"We'd better think fast!"

Gorgg's keys are clanking roughly in the lock now, and you know you must act.

If you want cast a spell to help you escape, turn to page 83.

If you prefer to say nothing about your powers and let Shaw attack the guard, turn to page 91.

I can't risk a display of my powers now, you think. *Who knows what Shaw would do once he discovered that I am a sorceress? Besides,* you think, *he is strong and able. He should be capable of handling this battle on his own.*

But your heart is gripped with fear as you watch the queen move in on Shaw. She has decided to tease him, using her prey to flaunt her power.

She pokes him with her antennae, and Shaw strikes back, cutting off a black fragment, making her hiss in rage. This time she pokes harder, knocking Shaw off his feet. He is up in a moment, his sword flying wildly, whipping off little pieces of antennae. The queen's anger is now uncontrolled.

She lets out a deafening war hiss, and suddenly, a thousand ants storm forward, swarming all over Shaw, all over you, and you feel hot stings on every part of your body.

The stingers are pricking at your skin like knives. You scream out in pain, wondering when the poison will take you, make you drowsy and weak.

You wonder what would have happened if you had decided to cast a spell. But it is too late, you feel consciousness slipping away. Shaw's eyes close, then yours, too. All is dark except the glowing embers of ant eyes.

THE END

"This is wild country, Shaw," you say, looking at the craggy trees that jut out over the river. You are making your way along a narrow bluff pass, cut through rocks and stumps and tangled, thorny brush.

"We're very close to Blissford Castle now," says Shaw. "That's where I was born. I haven't been back in fourteen years."

"Do you think the Yorguths have occupied it by now?" you ask.

"I don't think so. It's well-hidden among the trees," he says. "But we should approach with caution anyway—you never know what we might encounter."

Now you can see a great stone building ahead, perched right on the edge of the bluff. It is hidden on three sides by trees and heavy vines, and the cliff in front drops straight down to the crashing river.

You approach the castle cautiously, making your way across the weedy grounds. A few orange poppies and daylilies sprout here and there, evidence of past gardens.

"I don't hear a peep," says Shaw. He pushes open the great wooden door on the side, and you creep in, dust filling your nostrils.

"What a shambles!" says Shaw. "I suppose I should have expected it to be in this condition, with no one here to take care of it these many years."

Cobwebs and spiderwebs hang from the rafters, heavy wooden tables lie broken, panes of glass in the cathedral windows are splintered, the vines trailing inside, onto the walls and ceiling.

"Follow me," says Shaw. "I'll show you around." He takes you in and out of great, dusty rooms, the library, the dining hall, the bedrooms, and soon you

enter an empty room in which dusty red curtains have been ripped from the windows. A tall, carved chair is overturned in the middle, and an iron pot hangs over the stone hearth.

"The Throne Room," Shaw tells you. "I spent many hours playing in the corner while my father worked. I remember . . ."

His voice trails off, and he sinks to the floor beside the hearth. You see he is lost in thought, and you cross to the hearth quietly, to join him.

You sit silent for a long time, he in his own world, you in yours. Then you see his shoulders begin to tremble, and his hands move to his face, big angry fists digging hard into his eyes. He is crying, tears pouring through his fingers down his cheeks and onto his silken garments.

"Shaw," you say. But you stop, knowing that words will not soothe the pain. Your hand moves to his shoulder.

"I loved them," he murmurs. "Even though I was only five, I remember every detail—my mother's eyes, my father's smile. I can remember their voices and the sound of their laughter."

You sit silently, your eyes fixed on him.

"I dream about them sometimes. In my dreams, they stand and smile at me, as if they have come to kiss me good-night. They don't say a word. They just come to check on me, and then they disappear."

He shakes his head slowly.

"You can't know," he says. "You were lucky you don't remember your parents, that you were too little."

Anger rises within you. "That's not fair, Shaw," you say. "At least you have memories. I don't even have that. I don't even know who my parents were, if they were cruel or wonderful, if they loved me or never even wanted me . . ."

Now the tears pour from your eyes, tears of frustration that are hot on your cheeks. You lash out bitterly.

"Stop feeling sorry for yourself. At least you have something to dream of."

Your tears have stopped his abruptly. He turns to you, his eyes rimmed in red.

"You're right," he says quietly. "I'm sorry. I didn't mean what I said. When I dream about my parents, it makes me happy. I know they still care like they always did, and somehow, that protects me."

"I wish I could have that, Shaw. I only wish I knew who I was, who my parents were, that somewhere in my past was love, even just for a moment."

"Mialie," he whispers.

The sound of your name on his lips comforts you, quiets the pain. You sigh a long, soft sigh.

"I want you to make me a promise, Mialie," he says, looking down at his hands, still wet with tears. "I want you to promise that you will never forget me. No matter where our paths take us, I want to know that sometimes, even if you are old and gray, even if it's only in your dreams, that sometimes you will think of me."

"I shall never forget you, Shaw, Prince of Blissford," you say. "Of that you can be sure."

Shaw reaches over to take your hand in his.

"We don't have to go to the Cavern of Enchantment, Mialie," he says. "We could stay here and make this castle a home again. The Yorguths will never know this place is inhabited, it's hidden so well."

"But, Shaw, what about the message on the scroll?"

"What can the scroll do to overturn these barbarians? There will never be freedom in either kingdom. We may as well find a peaceful spot like this and live simple, quiet lives away from the Yorguth rule."

His grasp tightens around your hand, and you can hear the desperation in his voice.

"What do you think, Mialie? Will you stay here with me?"

What is your decision?

Stay and live with Shaw at Blissford Castle.
Turn to page 53.

Go on with your journey to the cavern.
Turn to page 141.

"I haven't got all day," snaps Waldemar. "Or is it night? Whichever. If you're just going to stand there, why . . ."

"Be patient, please," you say. You pull out your spell book, your eyes shooting daggers at the wizard. "This will take just a moment."

You shut your eyes, concentrating on the words to the Light Spell that worked so well on the goblins.

"Call your spell!" cries the wizard. "We do have rules to abide by, you know!"

You huff, exasperated, and announce, "Light Spell." In a moment, there is the same bright green flash that the goblins saw. The room is lighter than day. Waldemar and Shaw cover their eyes, squinting.

"There," you say, quite satisfied with your performance.

"A mere first-level spell," quips the wizard, deflating you. "Now watch this Flower Spell."

He clasps his wrinkled hands together and suddenly raises them high, when POOF! The floor of the cave comes alive with flowers. Gardenias and daffodils, poppies and lupine sprout from the cracks, their colors brilliant in the bright starlight. You stand in amazement, your eyes wide.

I'm not going to compliment him, you think. *He already has a good enough opinion of himself.*

"Well, if you think that's so marvelous," you say, using the same tone that Waldemar did after your Light Spell, "Watch this!"

You flip quickly through the pages of your spell book, certain that you have no spell that could outdo his. "How about this one?" you say. "Invisibility Spell."

After a few moments of concentration, POOF! The Wizard Waldemar has vanished in a puff of green smoke. You beam with pride.

"A mere second-level spell," comes a voice from the corner of the room. And with another POOF! the wizard is back, announcing, "Butterfly Spell!"

Instantly, the room flits with butterflies, butterflies everywhere, darting from flower to flower, lighting on your shoulders, swooping beneath Waldemar's stars. There are iridescent butterflies and speckled butterflies, butterflies of blue and emerald and crimson and black.

"That's quite a spell!" you exclaim, overwhelmed by the splendor.

"Then you admit you have lost?" he asks, bowing deeply, his beard buried in a flowerbed.

"Absolutely not!" you cry. "I'll make those butterflies disappear in a flash!" You know you have spoken too fast; you have no idea how to reverse the spell, and you will be forced to improvise.

"Watch this!" you say, bluffing. "Reverse Butterfly Spell!"

And with a great POOF! and a burst of green light, not a thing happens. Not one of the butterflies has disappeared.

You sigh in disappointment and turn to see a shiny green butterfly on your shoulder. Its beautiful gray eyes are looking right at you, and much to your surprise, the butterfly begins to talk.

"Thanks a lot, Mialie!" it says. "That was a very fine spell!"

"Shaw!" you cry. "Oh, Shaw, I've turned you into a butterfly! I had no idea . . ."

"Well, turn me back now, Mialie. Enough is enough!"

"But I don't know how!" you moan. Mortified at your rashness, you turn to Waldemar with a sheepish grin. "I could use your help in getting Shaw back, sir."

"A fine fourth-level spell," says the wizard. "But such irresponsibility, my little magician, is quite unacceptable. People like you are a disgrace to the profession. Pulling spells out of nowhere, and not having the power to reverse them! You should be ashamed!"

And you *are* ashamed. Your face goes dark crimson. "I don't know what to say," you admit.

"Then don't say anything!" snaps the wizard, making you feel worse. "Just let this little contest be a lesson to you. Your first duty to your gift of magic is responsibility. You are accountable for every spell, every action, every word. Engrave that in your heart, and then and only then will you deserve your gift."

You hang your head, humiliated. Not only have you embarrassed yourself in front of the wizard, but worst of all, in front of Shaw.

"You are not the only one at fault here," says Waldemar suddenly. He is pacing back and forth, his beard in his hands. "You were quite right about my pride. A terrible weakness it is, I must admit. Sometimes my pride does get in the way of my power. I should never have challenged you to the contest."

He looks so concerned, so miserable, that for a moment you feel very sorry for him. But in a flash, he is back to his bright self, saying, "Now then, we shall return your friend to his natural state, and call an end to this . . . this travesty."

With some mumbling and a great waving of hands,

the wizard changes Shaw back again, and he stands before you, safe and sound.

Waldemar drums his fingertips on his teeth. "Now, what in stars did you come to see me about in the first place?"

"Oh, that's right!" you say. "We certainly got off track!"

"We must get to the Cavern of Enchantment," says Shaw. "I wonder if you could point us in the right direction?"

"Why are you going to the cavern?" the wizard asks, his eyes narrowing.

"The wizard Junius sent his goldfinch with a scroll," you tell him. "He said it was urgent that I go immediately."

Waldemar strokes his beard with both hands, not taking his eyes from you for a moment. "And the scroll was delivered to you, little magician? Your name is not, by chance, Maria Analie, is it?"

"No," you say. "It is Mialie. And yes, the scroll was delivered to me."

"My, my, my," he says. He circles around you, eyeing you up and down. "So Junius sent you the scroll. And Mialie is your name."

He stops suddenly, as if struck by a thought. "And who is this traveling companion of yours?"

"Shaw is my name. Shaw of Blissford."

The wizard's eyes dart from you to Shaw and back again.

"And the jeweled sword you carry is no doubt the one and only Sword of Power."

Shaw nods.

"Well, I'll be!" exclaims Waldemar, as if he has just

put the last piece into a puzzle. "Then what are we waiting for? We must be off at once!" With a flick of his hand, Waldemar packs up his stars and empties the chamber of flowers and butterflies. "And I shall lead the way!"

"You're coming with us?" you ask, glancing at Shaw for a reaction. Shaw shrugs his shoulders.

"Absolutely!" cries the wizard. "There's a very evil, very nasty green dragon that guards the cavern at the cave exit, and I'd hate to see the two of you destroyed so soon.

"Onward!" he announces, tossing his beard over his shoulder. He hikes off toward the back exit, whistling a little tune.

"Come along, now!" he calls, and you are off.

Please turn to page 13.

"I'll go first," says Shaw, and he wriggles through the hole, with you right behind. The old man leaps up when you enter, but his foot snags on his beard and he topples back down.

"Oh, my heavens!" he exclaims, lying helplessly on his back, his legs and robe and beard all in a tangle. He sits up hastily, yanking his beard free, and sweeps his hand toward the ceiling, where little balls of light sparkle and shine. At his command they drop one by one into a pouch he is holding.

He smiles at you pleasantly, as though nothing unusual has occurred.

"I am W. W. Waldemar. And these," he says, shaking his bag, "are my stars."

"Pleased to meet you, Mr. Waldemar," you say. "And what does the W. W. stand for, may I ask?"

"World-Renowned Wizard," he answers. "Would you care to have a look at my stars?"

He opens his bag and the fiery balls shoot out again, until the entire roof is studded with stars, bright, white, and breathtaking.

"Night and day they shine, just for me. I've even created my own constellations," he brags, clapping his hands gleefully. "Isn't power marvelous?"

"Marvelous," you agree, exchanging an amused smile with Shaw.

"See that grouping over there?" the wizard continues. He points to a cluster in the shape of a man. "The WWW constellation, full of the finest new stars I could muster. And over there, we have Wizard Major, and next to it, Wizard Minor."

He stops, a sudden thought striking him. "You're not Yorguths, are you?"

"Far from it," says Shaw, laughing. "In fact, this young woman just happens to be a magician herself."

"No!" cries the wizard, thunderstruck. After a moment he asks, "Do you do stars?"

You are angry that Shaw has introduced the subject so lightly and shocked that the wizard thinks this is all some sort of game.

"No," you say quietly. "I don't do stars."

He looks relieved. "So what level are you, anyway?" he asks.

"Level, sir?"

"Well, of course. I mean, there are conjurers and enchanters, and mages and . . . Ouch!" A star has fallen on his beard, burning a hole right through it.

"A hazard of the profession," he explains, peeking at you through the hole. "Now take me," he continues. "I'm a twelfth-level wizard, high-powered and mighty.

"I spent many centuries of study before I became a true master of my powers. And now," he says, with a grand gesture toward the stars, "my name is written forever in the heavens."

You have had quite enough of his boasting. "Did you ever think that your pride may be even greater than your power?" you ask boldly.

The wizard glares at you, his eyes blazing brighter than his stars. "How dare you make such an accusation!" he booms. "What gives you the right to speak to me in such a fashion?"

"Well . . ." you stammer, "I suppose . . ."

"Since you are so self-righteous and bold, young magic-user," he cries, leaping to his feet, "then I suggest you put your magic where your mouth is!"

He draws out his spell book and slams it onto a table

of rock beside him. "I'm talking about a contest of magical powers. Lay down your book!"

"Contest?" you mutter, staring at his giant book, ten times the size of yours. "I don't really know . . ."

"I am not asking you!" he bellows. "I am commanding you! It is your duty as a magic-user to rise to the occasion and prove to others in the profession just what stuff you're made of!"

You shoot a glance at Shaw. He takes a step toward Waldemar, saying, "You don't understand, sir, that we have no time for this. We are in great danger of being attacked by goblins at any moment."

"Pshaw!" cries the wizard. "Goblins are no threat! They won't come within a hundred yards of me. They know I would destroy them in a flash. Now, to get back to our contest," he says, turning to you.

"I shall give you the advantage," says Waldemar. "You may use your spell book, but I shall cast my magic strictly from memory."

"But I haven't even agreed to—"

"You have no choice in the matter," states Waldemar flatly. "You go first. I'm waiting."

What are you going to do?

Fight a magic duel with the wizard.
If this is your choice, turn to page 70.

Or just leave your spell book in your pocket
and walk away? Turn to page 119.

Can't he tell how it hurts me to see him go? Doesn't he know I'm in love with him?

No, you think suddenly. *How could he? I've done nothing but hide my feelings since the first moment I met him. I must tell him now. I can't let him leave without his knowing.*

"Shaw," you say to him, your voice trembling. "Shaw, why are you leaving?"

His back is to you as he adjusts the few items in his knapsack. "What do you mean?" he says without turning around.

"Shaw," you stammer. "Don't you think . . . I mean, after all we've been through together, fighting off enemies and, talking about dreams, and . . . Shaw, don't you know that I'm in love with you?" you blurt out.

He spins around now, his eyes are shining, and his curls are fair and bright, and he looks wonderful in the moonlight, and you feel you have been very bold. You begin to regret speaking so openly.

Why would he want to stay with me? you think. *How foolish I must look to him!*

But you have no time to take your words back, for Shaw is rushing toward you now. He circles his hands around your waist and lifts you off the ground, whirling and twirling you in the air, round and round. You look at his face and it is beaming, just beaming.

"And how I love you, too!" he cries. "I was so afraid that now that you are a queen and I am but a prince, you wouldn't want me to stay. Oh, Mialie, you mean more than anything in the world to me!"

He sets you down and gazes into your eyes. "I do want to stay, Mialie." He holds your face in his hands and leans toward you, his lips meeting yours in a gentle kiss. Then he whispers, "I don't ever want to leave you."

You hug him tightly, burying your head against his chest, and you feel a rush of warmth and happiness to be so near to him.

Suddenly, Shaw takes a step back from you, his eyes big as stars.

"The scepter, Mialie!" he cries. "Look at the scepter!" It is glistening in the moonlight, the gems sparkling red and green and blue, and then you see it, and you draw in a gasp of air.

"It's the pearl, Shaw!" Like magic, the pearl at the top of the scepter floats into the air and embeds itself in the handle of Shaw's sword. The sword glows with a flaming green light, rises from its sheath, and hovers before Shaw, finally landing right in his hands.

"The sword has regained its power," says Shaw solemnly.

"And with it, you reign as the King of Blissford," you say.

"Yes," says Shaw, holding the sword tightly. "I am now the lawful King of Blissford. And you, Mialie, are the lawful Queen of Gallendale. Unless . . ."

"Unless what?" you ask.

"Unless, Mialie, we choose to unite our kingdoms. Unless we choose to become the King and Queen of Gallendale."

"Are you asking that we be wed, Shaw of Blissford?"

"That, Maria Analie, is exactly what I am asking."

"Well . . ." you hesitate, teasing him. "Will you expect to play your mandolin and dance beneath the

stars all the time?"

"Absolutely," he says, his face stubborn. "And will you expect to practice magic whenever you feel it necessary?"

"Absolutely," you answer.

"Then I'd say it's a fine match, wouldn't you?" says Shaw.

"Absolutely," you say.

Shaw wraps his arms around your waist, holding you tightly.

"About that dancing," he says. "I suggest a celebration dance is in order."

"That sounds wonderful. But we have no music."

"Ah, but we do," he says, his eyes sparkling. He begins to twirl you around and around. "Can't you hear it? Music. Everywhere. It's coming from my heart, Mialie. And that's where the best music of all is made."

"So it is, Shaw of Blissford," you say, your heart singing. "So it is."

THE END

"I'll try to put the dragonne to sleep," you say, digging into your pocket for your spell book.

But before you can even pull it out, the beast crashes the rest of the way through the door, howling and roaring, its yellow eyes flashing with rage.

Your legs give out beneath you, and you are too weak now to even reach for your spell book. All you can see is the gleaming of brass claws, the glimmer of great ivory fangs, and you are lost—lost in the deafening thunder of the dragonne as it roars its victory through the dark chamber of the Tower of Desolation.

THE END

I must try a spell, you think. *It is our only hope.* "I have a plan," you whisper to Shaw. "When Gorgg the guard returns, try to distract him for a minute or two. I need some time."

Shaw opens his mouth to protest, and you motion for him to be silent.

"Get up, prisoners!" growls Gorgg, his burly body looming above you. You see that he is armed with Shaw's sword. "Dawn lightens the sky, and your time has come." Thick leather straps hang from his hand, and he whips them against the stone wall with a sardonic smile.

You turn your back and pull out your spell book. You can hear Shaw strumming his mandolin, asking the guard to let him sing just one more song, one last song before he dies.

Your eyes scan the pages of the book quickly, and you find the Friend Spell, a spell that may be your salvation. *Why didn't I think of this one before?* you wonder. You read the words of the spell to yourself, and then spin around to face Gorgg.

Do it now, you say to yourself. *Look into his eyes and cast the Friend Spell.* Your eyes meet Gorgg's and you feel a surge of energy flowing between you.

Suddenly, his face softens, and he begins to wrap the leather straps sheepishly over his hand, saying, "I don't see why you must die for your deed. Ungaar is indeed a cruel lord." He shakes his heavy head and sighs.

"There is no reason," you agree quickly. "I meant no harm to anyone. All I ask of you is my freedom."

"And that you deserve," he says. "It is within my power to let you go. No one will accompany us to the riverbed. I'll pretend to attach the boulders to your ankles, but I will not tie the knot properly."

"And then we can swim free?" you ask.

"Yes," answers Gorgg. "Come, we must make haste before the other guards come to check on you."

With that, Gorgg grasps you and Shaw by the arms and leads you out the back entrance of the tunnel onto the riverbank. Thick, gnarled trees protect you from view should anyone in the Fortress glance in your direction.

Gorgg ties the boulders loosely to your ankles and and then says, "Go now. I'll push you into the water and you can swim away. And here," he says to Shaw. "Take your sword with you. Just do not breathe a word of this to anyone, or my life will be worthless."

"Not a word," you promise.

Gorgg pushes you off the riverbank, and the straps slip off as soon as you hit the water. You swim underwater, flowing with the current. Soon you are forced to come up for a breath of air.

The rush of the water is deafening. You can barely hear anything else, but suddenly, a loud bellow pierces the air, and you can make out a few words: "Stop . . . escaped . . . After them . . ."

The spell has ended, and Gorgg is screaming that you have escaped.

"Shaw!" you cry above the rushing water. "We must find a place to hide! It's the Yorguths!"

"Over there, Mialie! Get to the tower!"

You follow him as he hoists himself up out of the river, onto the shore. You crouch low, shivering in your wet clothes, and make your way through thorny thickets and over tangled tree roots.

Soon a gloomy tower, twisted with vines and branches, rises high above the treetops. You scramble behind Shaw, holding your skirt high, and soon plunge through a doorway into darkness.

"The Tower of Desolation," says Shaw.

"I can see why they call it that," you say, fighting your way through spiderwebs and past murky stone walls. You follow Shaw up a twisting, turning stairway to a chamber at the very top.

Shaw crosses to a narrow window and looks out. "They've sent their boats down the river after us," he announces. "They didn't see us come this way."

You breathe a sigh of relief and sink to the floor, pulling silky webs from your face. "Not the best," you say, looking around the tower chamber. "But it will do as a haven for the time being."

"It was a sturdy lookout tower before the Yorguths took over," says Shaw. "But like everything else, it was half-demolished by the barbarians and now stands desolate and utterly silent.

"But enough of that," he says, sitting down beside you. A sly glimmer comes into his eyes. "Now it's time to talk about you."

"What about me?" you ask, your stomach jumping uneasily.

"About the way you turned Gorgg around, what else?" he says. "You conceal your powers well, Mialie. I never would have suspected . . ."

"You never would have suspected that I was a witch, is that what you were going to say?" you snap.

Shaw's face darkens with a frown. "Not at all. Don't put words in my mouth. I never would have suspected you had such a marvelous gift. And I certainly wouldn't call it witchcraft. After all, you used it to save our lives."

"So I did," you say quietly.

"Don't you know that powers are neutral forces, Mialie? If you choose to be a witch, to use your powers toward an evil end, that's your decision. But it seems to me you've already decided otherwise."

"So I have," you say. "I've already chosen good."

"Do you know other spells, Mialie, more than the one you cast on Gorgg?"

"I know quite a few," you say. "I've studied my spell book since I was a child."

"I have a feeling you're a very powerful lady," says Shaw slowly. "More powerful than you may even suspect."

You are silent then, and you soon fall into daydreams about wizards and magic and caverns filled with moonlight. The next thing you know, Shaw is poking your shoulder.

"Mialie," he says, "it's time to move on."

You sit up, rubbing your eyes. "You mean I was sleeping? How late is it?"

"There's still some daylight left," he says. He opens the door to leave and lets out a gasp. Slamming the door shut again, he jumps back into the chamber, his hand flying to his sword.

Please turn to page 54.

"Ungaar has asked me to return to him," you say quietly. "And I have decided that I should."

"No!" cries Worm.

Shaw gasps in astonishment.

"He loves me," you continue. "He has always loved me, and I believe that with the power of the scepter and the power of my love, I can change his evil ways."

"But, Mialie," protests Shaw. "Do you love him?"

"My decision is made," you say flatly, not daring to look into Shaw's eyes. "I cannot be cruel enough to reject him now, when he needs me most."

You close your eyes, and a rush of darkness comes over you. It is as if a great door has shut somewhere within, leaving you trapped in deep, impenetrable blackness. *Have I chosen wisely?* you wonder. *Have I locked myself into a future where there is no hope?*

When you open your eyes, Shaw is standing at your side.

"I will not ask for your reasons," he says quietly. "Only you know if your decision is right for you. I just hope," he says, his voice laden with sadness, "I hope we shall meet again someday, Mialie."

He lifts his hands and runs his fingers gently through your hair. You see that his eyes are shadowed by the same untouchable darkness that you feel.

"And more than anything else in the world," he says, "I hope you will find happiness."

He leans down then and kisses your lips. There is a sweetness in the taste of his mouth, a sweetness tinged with great sadness, and you wish with all your heart that this were not a farewell kiss. You clutch the sleeves of his garments, tears welling in your eyes.

But I must think of Ungaar, you tell yourself. *It is*

he who needs me most right now. Shaw will find someone else, but Ungaar has no one but me.

You move away from Shaw and turn to Worm.

"Come, Worm," you say quietly. "Now we must return to Gallendale, and I must give Ungaar my response."

You follow the finch out of the cavern and away from Shaw. As you make your way along the pass, you wonder if you will ever be happy again. You wonder if you can truly change Ungaar's evil ways.

I still have time to reconsider, you think, sighing. For it is a long journey back to Ungaar's castle. Even longer when you are carrying with you the weight of a heavy heart.

THE END

Now you hear it, too—a low, hissing sound coming from behind the rocks. Then something begins to tickle the back of your neck, your wrists. You shiver, disturbed by this feeling in the darkness, and whip around to see that the entire cave wall is wriggling with long black antennae. The rocks seem alive, the giant antennae are growing longer, longer.

You back into the center of the shelter and see that now the whole cave is crawling with giant ants, huge golden ants with eyes red as fire, ants with tail segments that glow golden in the dark. They are coming from everywhere, their long black antennae twitching nervously. They race along the walls, leap from overhead rocks, searching, searching for prey.

"Shaw!" you cry in a panic. "Let's run!"

But as you hurry toward the entrance, you see her, and you stop dead in your tracks. It is the queen, an ant many times larger than the others, blocking the opening, her red eyes blazing. Her tail wriggles from one side to the other, its long sharp stinger glowing in the darkness of the cave. She is surrounded by warriors, who are slowly leading her toward Shaw.

"She'll poison you, Shaw!" you cry. "She'll sting you to death!"

Shaw's sword is flying now, whipping through the air in a blur, chopping segments off the warriors and leaving them scattered about the floor of the cave. The injured warriors grope about in the dark helplessly, but reinforcements are right behind, and Shaw's sword doesn't pause.

There are so many ants, ants everywhere, crawling and jumping, and the queen begins to make a hissing sound, low and angry.

I could put a spell on her, you think, *but then Shaw would know. He would know I am a sorceress. What would he think of me then? Perhaps he'd be so afraid, he'd even turn me over to the Yorguths.*

You must make a decision quickly. The ants are lining up behind the queen, swarming, swarming, all gold tails and red eyes, and Shaw is nearly to the back wall now, the queen just a few feet from him.

Will you let Shaw handle the battle alone?
If so, turn to page 64.

But if you decide to cast a spell on the ants,
turn to page 109.

Shaw plasters himself against the wall behind the door. The door flies open and Gorgg appears, a mammoth barbarian with huge arms and an evil glare in his eyes. His axe hangs by his side and he carries thick leather straps over his arm.

"Your time has come!" he growls.

Just then, Shaw jumps out from behind the door and seizes the Yorguth's axe from behind. He raises it high above his head and tries to strike the barbarian on the back. But Gorgg is fast and dodges the blade. He twirls around, and with a heavy blow of his fist, knocks the axe from Shaw's grip.

"You fool!" snarls Gorgg. He lunges at Shaw, knocking him against the wall, and with one great hand clutching the prince's throat, the Yorguth uses the other to wrap the leather straps around Shaw's legs and wrists.

"So you thought you'd outsmart this Yorguth, did you?" sneers Gorgg. He throws back his head and laughs coarsely. "You're nothing but a toy soldier to me. I'll throw you and the boulder into the river with one hand behind my back!" Shaw's eyes flash bright with anger, and your heart sinks. *Perhaps I should have considered a spell after all,* you think. *If I could get to my spell book without Gorgg discovering me . . .*

But the barbarian is lumbering toward you now, cracking the leather straps between his hands. And you begin to tremble with fear, for you know that you have reached . . .

THE END

"I think we should follow the markers, Shaw," you say. "That other passageway is so small, I'm afraid we might get stuck in it."

You make your way around the giant stalagmites and follow the markers into the passageway. The walls are oozing rusty droplets, and your feet squish along the flooded floor. An eerie shiver creeps up your spine as you breathe in the dank vapors.

"I don't like this part of the cave at all," you say as you pass beneath a jagged arch into another chamber. "Perhaps we should . . ."

But before the words are out of your mouth, wild howls pierce the dead silence of the cave. And they're coming closer!

"Yorguths!" you scream, spinning around to run back into the tunnel. With a rough jerk, something grabs you and you are thrown to the wet ground and dragged back into the chamber.

"I've got you now!" growls Buchfric, a huge barbarian who is Ungaar's prize warrior. His eyes blaze as he holds you to the floor. "We recognized the scraps of your skirt. Not a smart move, Mialie!"

You look at him with pleading eyes, hoping to soften his heart. "Please, Buchfric," you say.

But he throws back his head and lets out a wicked laugh. "Too late, Mialie. You are nothing but a common traitor to me now! When you cross Ungaar, you cross me."

You tremble and look away to see that Shaw, too, has been seized. The barbarians rip the torch and knapsack from him and hurl his mandolin to the floor. A huge Yorguth you know as Gorslak lifts an axe over his head and glares at Shaw, smiling cruelly.

"No!" you cry. "Don't! He did nothing wrong!"

"I'd love to see this delicate head on a platter!" growls Gorslak. "But our orders are to bring you both back alive." He lowers his axe and flings Shaw over his burly shoulder.

"Ungaar will be amused to have his property returned to him," snarls Buchfric, lifting you up with one arm. "It will give him great pleasure to punish you for betraying your Oath of Fealty."

He laughs loudly, and the other barbarians join in, howling with the triumph of their success.

As Buchfric lumbers down the passageways, through the dark, dank maze of the cave, you feel for your spell book.

It's still there, you say to yourself, *so all is not lost.* You know it is a long journey from the depths of the Caves of Gallendale to the Castle of Gallendale, where you will stand before Ungaar, with Shaw at your side.

You close your eyes, hoping you will think of a way to escape before you truly reach . . .

THE END

"Agreed," says Shaw, jumping off the stool. "You show me my sword, and you shall have your pot of gold."

The leprechauns dance about, clapping their hands with glee.

"Come along then," announces the little man with the pipe. He leaps to the ground and scurries off across the fields, followed by the rest of his band of small folk.

You and Shaw hurry behind, crossing hedges and streams, running uphill and downhill, panting and sweating trying to keep up with the quick little creatures.

At last you come to a great chestnut tree with a trunk huge and sturdy as a tower. The leprechauns lead you through a hole, and your mouth drops open at the sight inside.

In the flickering firelight, a great horde of treasure lies scattered about, glittering and sparkling. There are leprechauns everywhere you look, little men dancing about chests that overflow with bright treasures, little men playing golden harps, little men snug in corners counting gleaming gems and nuggets.

Shaw squints his eyes, perusing the bright riches. Suddenly, he lunges toward a treasure chest, grabbing for his sword.

But the leprechauns are too quick. In a flash, ten little men have seized the sword and scoot off to a far corner of the tree trunk. Mischievous laughter rings through the lair, and the leprechauns' eyes twinkle.

"So you thought you'd nab the sword and dash off, did you?" snickers the man with the pipe. "No such luck, my boy, no such luck. Not until we see that pot of gold."

Shaw's shoulders droop in frustration. He crosses to your side, whispering from the corner of his mouth. "Now what?" he says.

"These fine fellows have been so gracious to welcome us into their quarters," you say loudly, so the leprechauns can hear you. "I suggest we thank them by offering them some wine before we show them the pot of gold."

"But we have no wine," mumbles Shaw.

"Just give me the decanter in your knapsack," you whisper. Then you shout, "There's plenty of wine for all of them!"

Now the leprechauns are chattering excitedly among themselves. You know you have hit upon their great weakness. They love wine, and it will make them giddy and drowsy enough to numb their senses while you sneak over and nab the sword.

You take the water decanter from Shaw and turn your back so the little creatures cannot see the green glow that beams from the bottle as you cast your spell. In a flash, the water changes to deep red wine, and you spin around with a smile.

"Would any of you care for a taste of wine?" you ask brightly.

There is a mad dash of little feet as the leprechauns gather about. The fellow with the pipe is first in line, shouting, "How kind of you! By the way, I never introduced myself properly. I'm Tom, and I surely would enjoy a bit of a sip myself."

They pass the decanter among them, until every last drop is gone, and then Tom announces grandly, "And now I, too, shall share some spirits from my own cask with you, my friends."

He reaches into a heavy wooden chest and pulls out a clay pitcher brimming with more wine. "Gather about!" he says.

Soon the little creatures are reeling about dizzily. A few fiddlers begin to play, and the leprechauns skip and prance on their toes, singing bright, silly songs you've never heard before.

They guzzle still more of the spirits until they are so tipsy that they begin to topple into treasure chests and stumble face-down in piles of gold.

"Aren't you going to join us in the merrymaking?" slurs Tom. As he staggers toward you, he trips on his own feet and spills the rest of the wine into a box of jewels. "Oh, drat!" he exclaims, turning the empty pitcher upside-down over his head.

Shaw leaps to the corner then and seizes the sword, thrusting it into his sheath. He slips out the doorway, with you following behind, and not one leprechaun realizes you are gone.

"Good work!" cries Shaw. "Those arrogant little fellows certainly looked silly, didn't they?"

"And wait till they come to their senses and see what their merrymaking cost them!" you say, laughing. "They'll be furious!"

Please turn to page 130.

"I'll go first," you say. Shaw helps you out the tiny window and you descend the rope slowly, watching for any sign of movement in the courtyard. All is still, and soon you and Shaw are back in the valley, walking through the moonlit grasses, dotted purple and yellow with wild flowers.

"Here's the mountain shelter I told you about," he says, climbing up the mossy rocks on a hillside. You follow him and are soon in the darkness of a small cave, completely protected from view. It is cool inside and very tranquil. He stretches out on a flat rock, his head leaning against the cave wall, and begins to strum his mandolin.

"Well, do you want to hear it?" he finally asks. He seems to be feeling a little embarrassed.

"Yes," you say. "I'd like to hear it."

"I've never sung it out loud before," he apologizes. "I mean, I don't know how good it is."

"I'm sure it's wonderful," you say. "Please, I really want to hear it, Shaw."

His voice quivers a little from shyness, but his fingers are confident on his instrument, plucking clear, pure tones in the darkness.

O my voyaging heart
Was used to farewells
Till the day I first saw you.
I long to wander inside
Your golden-green eyes
So soft and clear as the dew.
How I dream now, milady,
That my travels shall cease
I pray, never bid me adieu.

You are barely breathing, listening to the words. His nonchalance seems to have melted away, and he is touching and real. *Who are you, Shaw, Prince of Blissford?* you want to say. *Who are you deep inside?*

When he has finished, he leans back against the cave wall again, drumming his fingertips on the wood of his mandolin.

"I don't make much of a prince, do I?" he says quietly. "Here I am, singing love songs and wandering like a nomad."

"I think you're a fine prince myself," you say. "And I really liked the song, Shaw."

He goes on with his train of thought. "You know the sword I carry? It was my father's. It's the Sword of Power for the Kingdom of Blissford, Mialie." He pauses and sighs heavily. "Only, it's powerless. There's a pearl missing from its handle, and without the pearl, the sword is worthless. Rather like a prince without a kingdom, I suppose."

"Where do you think the pearl is?" you ask.

"Lost or hidden somewhere in the kingdom, probably. That's what drives me to look into willow tree holes and such," he says, laughing. "Maybe someday it will turn up."

"And then the sword would give you the power to rule the Kingdom of Blissford, wouldn't it?" you ask.

"Yes," says Shaw quietly. "I would have the power to overturn the Yorguths."

After a while he says, "And now you know my dream, Mialie. What about you? What's your dream?"

An emptiness floods your insides. *Here is Shaw, a born prince, with dreams of kingdoms and swords of great power,* you think, *and who am I but an orphan with strange powers of sorcery, and very small dreams, so insignificant?* You wish this conversation had never begun, you wish you had an extraordinary story to share, you wish you could jump up and run out of this secret cave shelter.

Then suddenly you shake your hair back over your shoulders. *I'm not going to apologize for who I am,* you think. *Why should I?*

"I was abandoned as an infant and raised by the Yorguths," you say. "Living with barbarians, it's hard for me to imagine possibilities, dreams that could come true."

"Mialie," Shaw says softly. "What is life, with no dreams? There must be something, deep in your heart, that you want."

"I want to be free to be myself," you say. "I want to learn about . . ." *About my powers,* you were going to say, but you stop. "I want to learn who I really am, Shaw. That is my dream."

"And once that dream becomes real, Mialie . . ." Shaw suddenly leaps to his feet, his sword drawn.

"What is it?" you cry.

"I heard something behind those rocks," he whispers. "Move over against the wall, Mialie. Quick!"

You pin yourself to the opposite wall, holding your breath.

Please turn to page 89.

You and Shaw head back down the passageway to the dragon's chamber.

Just outside, Shaw turns to you and whispers, "I'll distract the beast by offering to surrender my sword. You weave the spell."

Fear stabs you, and you begin to tremble, knowing that Shaw will be in great danger.

"Please be careful, Shaw," you whisper.

He gently lifts your chin and looks into your eyes. "I will, Mialie," he says, and then he is gone.

"So, you have returned for further punishment," growls the dragon, as Shaw stands before it, Waldemar still imprisoned in its claw. "Or have you decided to abandon your efforts to free this insignificant conjurer from my grasp?"

"Your power is too great," says Shaw, raising the sword, its jewels gleaming in the light of his torch. "We have no hope but to offer you the Sword of Power."

The dragon's fiery eyes focus on the sword, the monster's greed distracting its attention from you as you step inside the chamber and concentrate on the words of the spell.

There's a FLASH! and a golden ball of light streaks from your hands into the dragon's eyes, and the monster howls in pain, throwing its great green head from one side of the cave to the other.

"How dare you blind me!" it roars, its tail whipping and limbs flying. Suddenly, it opens its claws, sending Waldemar to the ground with a crash.

Shaw scrambles over to the wizard and picks him up, throwing him over his shoulder.

"Run!" you shout, racing back toward the passageway, and Shaw, laden with Waldemar, is close behind.

Suddenly, the dragon opens its mouth and breathes a huge cloud of green gas into the room.

"Hold your breath, Shaw!" you cry, not daring to breathe in the poisonous gas. The cloud is moving toward you when you reach the exit. You spin around and grab the torch from Shaw, hurling it back into the chamber.

"Run, Shaw!" you scream. "Run for your life!"

There is an explosion behind you then, a thunderous burst, and you glance back to see great flames pouring from the chamber.

"For once, the dragon's evil backfired on it," you say with satifaction.

Soon the passageway opens into a small cave, overgrown with vines and mossy vegetation. The mouth of the cave is large, and bright sunlight streams through the trees and flickers on the rocks.

"Sunlight!" you cry. "It's so wonderful to see sunlight again!"

"Yes," says Shaw. He props Waldemar against the rocks and begins to collect leaves and grass. "I'll make a bed for him," he says. "He's still unconscious."

You sit beside Waldemar, feeling helpless. "I wish there were something I could do for him," you say. "But I don't know any spells that would revive him."

You lean your head against a rock, scanning the area for a sign of your goal, the Cavern of Enchantment. All you see is this small cave, very ordinary, and the tangle of woods along the bluff beyond. Your heart is heavy with disappointment.

"You look so downcast, Mialie," says Shaw, arranging the leaf-and-grass bed. "What's wrong?"

"I thought the cavern was supposed to be here,"

you say wearily. "I don't see a sign of it anywhere."

"I don't know what you expected," says Shaw, "but this is it—the Cavern of Enchantment. No different from any other rock formation in the kingdom."

"But how can that be?" you cry, jumping to your feet. Suddenly, a strange rock catches your eye. It is shaped exactly like a person lying on its side.

"Shaw," you whisper, clinging to the cavern wall. "Is that a Yorguth?"

"A Yorguth it is," he says. "A Yorguth turned to stone."

Now you see that they are scattered throughout the cave, many statues, overturned and vine-covered. They are all shaped like Yorguths, preserved forever, their tangled hair and angry faces pure stone.

"Then, according to the stories you heard, this must be the cavern," you say. "But I don't see a sign of enchantment, other than these petrified Yorguths."

"You know as well as I, Mialie," says Shaw, "that enchantment is not always visible to the eye."

"That's true," you say. "But I don't feel anything unusual, Shaw. Let me take a look at the scroll."

Shaw pulls out the parchment, and you read the message again:

The moon at midnight will reveal
Your secret destiny there.

You feel your heart racing with excitement again. "We have to wait until midnight, Shaw," you say. "I wonder just what's going to happen then."

"I don't know," says Shaw. "But what I DO know is that I need a few hours' rest in the meantime. It's been a long journey."

"Rest?" you cry. "How can you rest at a time like

this? I'd be afraid we'd sleep straight through till morning!"

But Shaw is already curling up against the rocks. You fight to stay awake, but your lids are heavy, and soon you stretch out next to Waldemar.

"I'll just close my eyes for a moment," you tell yourself. "Just for a short rest . . ."

You are asleep within seconds, wandering through heavy darkness in your dreams. Suddenly, your dream brightens, and you feel yourself floating in a white, haunting light.

You wake up abruptly and bolt to your feet. Through an opening in the roof of the cavern, the moonlight is streaming, bright and white as the mid-day sun. The light fills the cave with brightness, everywhere illuminating rocks carved with inscriptions.

"Shaw!" you cry. "Wake up and look at this!"

He is awake and on his feet in a moment, his eyes wide with amazement.

"The writing is Gallenian!" you cry. "That language hasn't been used for many years, not since the Yorguths took over."

"Can you use your powers to read it?" asks Shaw, bursting with curiosity.

"Just give me a minute to concentrate," you say, closing your eyes. Your hand glides over the stones, and in a moment the scribblings are as legible as your own tongue.

The moonlight is brightest on a great stone to your left, and you begin to read, your heart quickening at this moment of discovery.

The Princess Maria Analie is stolen
This very day from her cradle
By Ungaar of the Yorguths.
In exchange for her life,
We sacrifice ourselves and our Kingdom.

"Shaw," you say, barely breathing. "Isn't that the name Waldemar asked about? He wanted to know if it was my name."

"Maria Analie," Shaw repeats. "It does sound a lot like Mialie. Could it be your birth name?"

"I . . . I don't know," you say.

"Well, keep reading!" cries Shaw. "Maybe the messages will tell us!"

The moonlight has drifted to the east, uncovering more writing on a rock in the center of the cavern. You step over to the rock, place your hands on the carvings, and read:

Your gift, Maria Analie,
Is a power far greater than ours.
You alone can destroy the evil Ungaar
And restore freedom and goodness
To the Kingdom of Gallendale.

"Do you think Waldemar was right, Shaw? Is it possible that I truly am . . ." you begin, but disbelief keeps you from continuing.

"It is not only possible," comes a voice from behind, "but it is most certain that you, Mialie, are the Princess Maria Analie of the Gallenian messages."

"Waldemar!" you cry. "You're all right!"

"Great heavens, yes," he says, smoothing out his beard as he rises to his feet. "But this is no time to discuss me and my health. Read on, my child. I have not witnessed a marvel such as these messages in centuries!"

You turn back to the carvings, and your eyes grow wider as the moonlight moves downward to a rock on your right. There is a tiny handprint, that of an infant, embedded in the rock. Above the handprint is an inscription:

The Scepter of Power beneath this rock
Can be removed by one handprint alone:
That of Maria Analie.
Use its power well, Fair Princess,
That Gallendale be regained.

"It is signed 'The King and Queen of Gallendale,' " you say, your voice faint. Your hand trembles as you place it over the tiny print.

You watch, your heart frozen in amazement, as the rock slowly moves from the base of the cavern wall. A glow of light bursts forth from behind the rock.

There lies a long scepter of gold, inlaid with emeralds and rubies, crowned with a great pearl. You reach down and take the long, ornate rod into your hand. Suddenly you are filled with brightness, and you feel a lifetime of heaviness lifting from within you.

Then, you watch in wonder as the great pearl from the scepter's handle rises into the air. It hovers above you for a moment, hung in a soft cloud of green. Then it floats toward Shaw and descends slowly, finally embedding itself in the empty setting in the handle of his sword.

Shaw cries out, and the cavern is filled with a great flash of green, surrounding his Sword of Power.

"The power has been returned," says Shaw, his voice shaking with amazement. "And with this power," he says, lifting his sword high, "shall I rule Blissford."

"You shall never rule Blissford," bellows a voice from outside the cavern. "For Blissford and Gallendale belong to me alone!"

You spin around, your heart trembling, and stand face-to-face with Ungaar. His sword is drawn and his eyes blaze with rage and madness. He is surrounded by a band of Yorguths, faces fierce, axes in hand.

"You have betrayed me, Child of Sorcery," he screams. The moonlight plays on his twisted face, making it glow hideously. "And for that, you and your foolish companions shall die!"

You grasp the scepter tightly in your hand. *I have the power now,* you remind yourself.

"It is you, Ungaar of the Yorguths," you say quietly, "who shall die. Goodness shall prevail, and evil shall be destroyed."

A burst of cruel laughter spills from his mouth. "And how do you intend to destroy me?" he howls. "With that useless scepter of yours? Do you think your little ornament can stand against me and my great army?"

The Yorguths behind him howl with laughter, and beat their shields with their horrible axes. Panic fills your heart. You know the scepter is powerful, but you don't know how to use it. *Should I cast a spell with it?* you wonder. *Or should I wield it like a sword? Can I, Mialie, really control its power?*

"Don't let him intimidate you," whispers Waldemar. "Trust the inscriptions, Maria Analie. It is you who have the power to destroy this evil lord."

"Your time has come, traitor," Ungaar sneers as he walks toward you. "And I shall plunge this sword straight into your heart."

You have no time left. What will you do?

Do not trust the scepter's power;
instead, ask Waldemar to cast a spell on Ungaar.
Turn to page 137.

Trust the power of the scepter and point it
at Ungaar. *Turn to page 152.*

I can't worry about Shaw's reaction, you think. *Our lives are in danger and I must use my powers. I will destroy the queen ant with a Burning Light Spell.*

"Move out of the way, Shaw!" you cry, leaping in front of him toward the queen ant. You pronounce the words of the spell, and suddenly, a flash of light, a terrific bright green flash, shoots from your fingertips straight toward the queen ant.

"What in the world!" you hear Shaw yell. Slowly the light dissipates, and you see the queen, burned and shriveled up in a ball on the cave floor. The warrior ants scatter, running helplessly here and there, lost without their leader. Soon they retreat into the crevices in the walls of the shelter, and you turn to Shaw, not knowing what to expect.

He has a wide, bright, astonished smile on his face, and you can see the flash of his white teeth even in the dimness of the cave.

"Mialie, why didn't you tell me?" he says, positively astounded.

"You mean I've caught you off guard, Prince Shaw?" You pretend to be confident, but your insides are churning, afraid of what he is thinking, afraid that he shares the Yorguths' hatred for magic.

"Off guard!" he says, still in shock. "Try impressed, amazed, flabbergasted . . . "

"What about afraid, Shaw?" you venture to ask. "Aren't you just a little afraid of what you just saw?"

"Not at all. Not a bit," he says. "I'm just thoroughly surprised, and as I said, impressed. You've got one fine power there, Mialie, and I want to know where it came from."

"As a matter of fact, Shaw, so do I," you say, now

quiet. You've revealed your worst secret, so you may as well tell him everything. "You see, Shaw, I never knew who my parents were, if they were wizards or sorcerers, if they were good or bad. I was afraid of how you would react to my spell, because . . . well . . . I've always assumed my powers were evil."

"What made you think that?"

"I don't know. Ungaar, maybe. If he ever knew what happened here just now, I'd be executed as fast as that queen ant shriveled from the Burning Light Spell."

"Don't you know that powers are neutral forces, Mialie? You make of them what you want. If you want to be an evil sorceress, that's your decision. But if you choose to use your gift wisely . . ."

"Of course," you interrupt. "That's what the scroll said: 'Trust your powers rare.' It meant I should stop fearing my magic. It's not an evil force after all!"

Feeling wonderful about yourself and your powers, you suddenly bound off, over the queen ant and out of the shelter, your skirt flying about you.

"Come on, Shaw," you call. "I'm very anxious to get to the cavern now. I know there's something of great importance waiting for me there."

You listen for Shaw's footsteps behind you, but you don't hear a sound. You glance back to see if he's following, and your mouth opens in a silent moan.

Please turn to page 30.

"Quick!" you cry. "Let's take the passageway ahead!"

You race through the opening into a tunnel, and to your surprise, you see light at the far end. You hurry toward the light, soon leaving the howls of the goblins echoing in the chamber behind.

"Daylight!" you cry happily, as you exit from the passageway. The brightness is nearly blinding, and you squint hard until your eyes adjust. "Hurry!" you say. "Take out the map, and let's see where we are."

Shaw sets his knapsack down on the ground, and snuffs out his torch in the dirt. You pull out the map, examining it closely.

"It looks as if we took this exit," you say. "We're back in the valley again."

"Now I've got my bearings," says Shaw. "We should head due south from here, I'd say."

"That's how it looks on the map," you say, glad that Shaw and the map are in agreement. You pack up your things and head off down the valley.

"We're lucky we got out of those caves with our heads and our belongings," you say.

"For a while I was worried the goblins might get my sword," says Shaw. "And I can't afford to lose that!"

"It's a beautiful sword, Shaw. How did you happen to come upon it?" you ask.

"It was my father's," he says, running his fingers over the jewels in its handle. "It's the Sword of Power for the Kingdom of Blissford."

You gasp in astonishment, your eyes big as stars. "You mean that sword carries the power to overturn the Yorguths?"

"Someday it will," says Shaw. "But there's a pearl missing from its handle. Without it, the sword is useless."

You start to walk again. "Then it's like the Scepter of Power for the Kingdom of Gallendale," you say. "Until the rightful heir to the throne finds it, the Yorguths will remain in power."

You walk on in silence, contemplating the sword and the scepter, and as the sun begins to set, you enter a woods of pines and birches. You breathe deeply of the mossy forest smells, a great relief after the dank mustiness of the caves.

"Shaw," you say, "do you think . . ." You freeze dead in your tracks.

Please turn to page 30.

Shaw hurries up the ladder, and you follow close behind. Soon you are standing in a tiny room, beamed in oak branches, and very simply furnished. There is a peg bed in the corner and an oaken table with two chairs in the middle of the room. The window sill is lined with clay jars and vessels.

"There's no one here," you say, a bit relieved. "I think we should go."

"Wait a second, Mialie," says Shaw, determined to get to the bottom of the dagger message. He crosses to a large box by the window and opens it slowly, his face suddenly beaming.

A soft, feminine voice comes from inside the box: "So you have found me at last."

"Who are you?" asks Shaw, eyes glued to the box.

"They call me Adriana the tree sprite," says the voice, smooth as silk. "And what do they call you, young fighter with the moonlit eyes?"

You glare at the box, still unable to get a glimpse of this tree sprite.

"I am called Shaw," he answers.

The creature rises from the box, and Shaw's eyes are fixed upon her, spellbound. Her blond hair tumbles over her shoulders like a cascade, and long lashes fringe her violet eyes. You wish you had worn something prettier than your homespun skirt, for this tree sprite is lovely in her filmy white dress, its hem laced with flowers.

"I think we'd best leave now, Shaw," you say in the most pleasant voice you can muster.

"Who is she?" demands the sprite, eyeing you disdainfully.

"I'm Mialie," you snap. "And this 'young fighter

with the moonlit eyes' is traveling with me."

"I want her to leave," Adriana tells Shaw. "My wonders are for you alone."

Shaw looks at you blankly and turns back to Adriana. She smiles sweetly at him and lifts her hand to twist one of his curls playfully. "Hair like sunbeams," she says.

"Shaw," you repeat, speaking slowly and clearly. "It is time to leave."

But Shaw is mesmerized by the violet eyes of the creature, and he doesn't budge. The sprite shoots you a nasty look from beneath her long lashes. She plucks a white flower from the hem of her dress and places it into Shaw's hair, just over his ear.

"Ask the girl to leave," she urges sweetly. "You and I have wonders to explore, odes to sing, marvelous worlds ahead of us."

"She is dangerous, Shaw," you warn. "She will charm you if you let her."

But Shaw is lost in her violet eyes, and you must decide what you want to do. You have two choices:

You can put a spell on Adriana. If that is your choice, turn to page 145.

Or pull Shaw's sword and threaten Adriana. Turn to page 127.

"Quick, Shaw!" you cry. "Attach your rope to the window. It's our only way out of here!"

Shaw's fingers fly, fastening the knots, and you watch as the dragonne, with one final blow, crashes through the door.

"Go, Mialie!" screams Shaw. "I'll get my sword and come down after you!"

"No, Shaw!" you cry, as you squeeze out the window. "Leave your sword! The beast will kill you!"

But Shaw does not listen. As you descend the rope, you hear another thunderous roar echo through the chamber. Your whole body shudders, and you let yourself down quickly, the roughness of the rope burning your hands. You leap from the end of the rope down into the brush.

"Shaw!" you scream. "Shaw! Are you all right?"

Then you see him scramble out the window and down the rope.

With a THUMP! he lands in the bushes by you.

"Let's go!" he hollers, pushing himself to his feet. He seems a bit unsteady, shaken from the fall.

You pull your skirt from the tangled brush and make your way behind him through the woods. Soon he comes to a stop and turns back toward you.

"We're out of danger now, Mialie," he says. "The dragonne won't pursue us. It never leaves its own territory unless it's in danger."

"Why did you go back for your sword, Shaw?" you ask. "It could have meant your life."

"My sword is very important to me, Mialie," he says. "It was my father's. It's the Sword of Power for the Kingdom of Blissford."

You gasp in astonishment.

"Don't be too impressed," he says. "A pearl is missing from its handle, making it powerless. Only if I find the pearl will I have the power to rule Blissford as the rightful king."

He is quiet for a moment, and then he runs his hand through his curls. "I'm exhausted, Mialie," he says.

"And I'm famished!" As you say it, you realize that the sun is setting behind the silhouettes of the trees. "No wonder," you add. "We've barely eaten all day!"

"Let's stop at the village of Telton for a bite," says Shaw. "It's just a mile east of the river."

You follow him away from the bluff and out of the trees, toward an expanse of golden wheat fields. Soon a town appears, its clay-roofed houses huddled together as if they are one big building.

There is a great bell clanging as you approach, and the noise of talking and laughter lifts high above the roofs and drifts toward you. You wind down a narrow cobblestone street into the square. The vendors are closing up, taking down colorful striped tents, packing their wares into crates.

"I've never seen anything like this, Shaw!" you exclaim. "Such activity, such excitement! The village of Gallendale seems dull compared to this."

"Let's eat at the inn here," says Shaw, stopping before a great stone house with a wooden sign swinging above the door. "Inn of the Black Boar," it reads. The smell of food floats out and fills your nostrils.

"You don't think there will be any Yorguths here, do you?" you ask.

"There shouldn't be. They'd rather demolish towns than enjoy them."

Inside the inn, it is hazy and loud. Noisy groups of people crowd about the long tables, talking and enjoying the mounds of food in front of them. You make your way through the sea of tables to sit in the corner.

"I'm starving," Shaw tells the big aproned woman who comes to your table. "We'll both have some of your broth and two loaves of black bread."

"Two loaves!" you cry. "I'm hungry, but . . ."

"One for us, one for the knapsack," he says. Then he turns back to the woman and orders a decanter of water. "For the journey," he says to you.

Soon steaming bowls of broth sit before you, heaped with chunks of mutton and carrots. Your mouth is full of carrots when a girl at the next table cries, "Well, if it isn't Shaw of Blissford!" Her black curls frame her rosy cheeks, and her eyes dance excitedly. "Well, well, Prince Shaw. I'd given up on you ages ago!"

"This is Bethany," Shaw tells you, leaning over to

kiss her hand. "And this is Mialie," he says. The girl completely ignores you. She takes Shaw's hand and holds it tightly.

"Oh, Shaw, you look just wonderful. Tell me about all your adventures. What great monsters have you captured with that sword of yours?"

Bethany is gazing into Shaw's eyes, spellbound. You swallow a hunk of mutton, and it sticks in your throat. Snatching up your cup, you gulp some water to wash it down.

"No monsters of any consequence," Shaw is saying. "Just a few goblins here and there."

"And a few maidens, I suppose!" says Bethany with a wink. She begins to laugh, her teeth white as pearls.

Soon Shaw is so engrossed in Bethany that he has turned his back on you, and he is laughing, and she is laughing, and you set down your spoon, unable to eat a another bite.

You sit, beet-red and humiliated to have them ignoring you. Anger seethes gradually through your body. *I don't have time for this nonsense!* you think.

Now Shaw is telling a mildly funny story, and Bethany is howling with glee.

"Oh, you're so funny, Shaw!" she cries.

Oh, you're so funny, Shaw! you fume. *Well, I'm not going to sit here and take this!* And so you:

Leave the inn and head for the cavern alone.
If this is your choice, turn to page 43.

Cast a spell on Bethany to make her look foolish.
If you want to try this, turn to page 32.

You march straight up to the wizard, your hands on your hips.

"Mr. Waldemar," you say. "This is no game. My magic powers are not to be used for sport. I refuse to involve myself in such a contest."

For a moment his eyes blaze with anger, and you are afraid he may turn you into a worm. But then he begins drumming his fingertips on his bottom lip, saying, "You are very wise, young magician. Very wise."

He paces back and forth, his beard in his hands. "Sometimes I think my pride is greater than my power. A terrible weakness, terrible. It was most irresponsible for me to challenge you to that contest. You were right to decline."

Your jaw drops open. "Is that a compliment?"

"Of the highest level," answers Waldemar, crossing to place a hand on your shoulder. "In fact, I am ashamed that you, a magic-user so young and fresh, have wisdom beyond my own. I see that you have a great respect for your powers, and that is the first and foremost quality in a great enchanter."

You beam with pride, glancing toward Shaw, who is smiling broadly.

"Now what brought you here in the first place?" asks the wizard.

"We are on our way to the Cavern of Enchantment, and we need directions," you say.

The wizard takes his hand from your shoulder and stares at you. "Why would you want to go to the cavern?" he asks.

"The wizard Junius sent me a scroll directing me to go immediately."

Waldemar's eyes grow big as stars and he stares at

you, spellbound. "You received the scroll? It was sent to you?"

"Why, yes," you answer.

"And what did you say your name is?"

"Mialie, sir."

"Short for Maria Analie?" he asks, still intent.

"I wouldn't know, sir," you say slowly, intrigued by the wizard's excitement.

"And your companion here, who is he?" Waldemar asks.

"I am Shaw of Blissford," Shaw offers.

"Aha! exclaims the wizard. "I've no doubt then that the sword you carry is the Sword of Power."

"That is true," says Shaw. "But how do you know that?"

"You'll know soon enough," says Waldemar, suddenly very busy waving his arms about and packing up his stars. "I shall take you to the cavern. There is a green dragon that guards the entrance, and you could use my help fighting it."

"That's not necessary . . ." Shaw begins, but you grasp his arm to silence him.

"He seems to know something about the scroll and the cavern," you whisper. "Let's follow him."

The wizard is already hiking out a back exit you hadn't noticed before, tossing his beard over his shoulder.

"Well, come along!" he yells, his voice echoing down the tunnel. "No dillydallying! You are traveling with World-Renowned Wizard Waldemar and I shall see that you get to the cavern quick as a flash!"

Please turn to page 13.

"Bring the sword to us, and the pot of gold will be waiting here upon your return," you say.

Shaw looks at you, relieved. You see that he trusts that you have a plan in mind.

"And how can we be certain you will return with my sword?" Shaw asks the little fellow with the pipe.

"Why, come along with us, my boy," says the leprechaun, blowing a smoke ring. "She can get the gold while we're gone. But I want you to swear that we will be satisfied that the pot of gold is more valuable than the jewels in the sword."

"Yes," you say quickly. "You won't be disappointed."

"Then we're off!" cries the little man, leaping down from the tree.

"Just a minute, Shaw," you say. "Leave your knapsack with me." The leprechaun shoots you a suspicious look. "I'm . . . I'm rather hungry and could use a bite of the bread in your pack," you stammer.

"Of course," says Shaw, handing the pack to you.

The leprechauns scurry off across the hills, rubbing their greedy little hands in delight. "Good luck!" Shaw whispers to you and then races off behind them.

I may just need it, you think. Your eyes scan the woods to be certain no leprechauns are left. *They may still be invisible,* you think. You murmur the words of a spell that detects invisibility, but no one is evident. They've all gone to their lair.

You unfasten the knapsack and pull out all the metal items. There is a dagger, a tinderbox, a small flask, and some tools. You pile them into a heap.

Then you open your spell book, and pronounce the words of your Fool's Gold Spell. POOF! Streaks of green flash from your fingertips, turning the objects into a pile of shimmering, glittering gold pieces. You snap your book shut, pleased with your success.

Just in time, you think. For the leprechauns are returning.

"We want gold! Give us gold!" they chant as they dance into the grove of trees. When they see the gleaming pile of treasure, their eyes nearly jump from their heads, and they fall into silence.

"Give Shaw his sword and you may have the gold," you tell them.

"Just a moment," says the spokesman, puffing on his pipe. "I must be certain this is no trick."

He pulls a tiny jeweler's pick from his vest pocket and taps one of the gold pieces. A sigh of relief escapes you when he smiles with satisfaction, pleased with the indent in the soft metal.

"You may give him his sword now," says the leprechaun. "And we'll haul our new treasure back and have ourselves a fine celebration!"

The little men dive toward the golden pile, and you and Shaw hurry away as fast as you can.

"Was that real gold?" asks Shaw.

"Fool's Gold," you confess. "And I'd hate to be anywhere near those leprechauns when they discover they've been duped."

Shaw laughs a great, hearty laugh. "Those greedy fellows deserve it, for stealing my sword."

Please turn to page 130.

I know this spell by heart, you think, your head fuzzy from the knock. *I must concentrate . . .*

Then you mumble the words and FLASH! A terrific blaze of green light bursts through the room, filling every nook and cranny in the cave. You squint from the brightness, covering your eyes with your hand.

Now the goblins are howling in ugly voices, running off in all directions, blinded by the light. They slam into walls, into each other, swinging their swords and spears frantically.

Using the quarreling and yowling of the goblins as cover, you and Shaw run into another chamber.

You race down shadowy tunnels, in and out of nasty-smelling chambers, leaving the howls and curses of the goblins behind. Soon all is silent.

"We're out of danger now," you say, sinking down on a damp boulder to catch your breath. You close your eyes, but your mind is racing. You are so worried about what Shaw will say about the spell. When you open your eyes again, he stands before you, staring.

"What are you staring at, Shaw of Blissford?" you snap, planting your hands on your hips. *He's probably scared to death of me now,*you think.

"At you, Mialie," Shaw answers quietly.

"Well, you needn't be so obvious about it. After all, we did escape the goblins, didn't we?" you cry, jumping to your feet and pacing back and forth.

"Mialie," says Shaw. "Calm down."

"Don't you tell me what to do. I will calm down when I choose!" you exclaim. But inside, you say, *I shouldn't have done it! We could have escaped without my magic, and now I've ruined the start of a fine relationship.* You feel empty and miserable.

"And furthermore," you spit, "will you stop staring at me? What's the matter? Are you afraid I'll turn you into a grasshopper? Or maybe a centipede?"

"Stop it, Mialie!" he bursts out. "Just stop it!" His tone is so harsh that for a moment you nearly burst into tears. "Now tell me why you're so upset."

You lift your chin defiantly. "I'd say that's rather obvious," you answer. "Now you know the truth."

"What do you mean, the truth?" he asks.

"Now you know, Shaw of Blissford, that I'm a witch, a sorceress who keeps her secret hidden in her heart and in her little black book. There, are you satisfied now?" you cry.

"But you have a great gift, Mialie," Shaw says. "I'd give my eye teeth for powers like yours."

"Don't humor me, Shaw," you say crossly, sinking back down on your boulder. In a flash, Shaw sits beside you. He grasps both your shoulders and shakes you firmly.

"Listen to me, Mialie," he says. "It's unfortunate that the Yorguths equate magic with witchcraft. It's only because they are ignorant people. They fear magic, and the terrible thing is that they've taught you to fear it, too."

You sit in silence, unable to say a word.

"You have the power to use your magic in whatever way you choose, for good or for evil. The power itself is neutral. You decide how to use it. Understand?"

You look down at your feet, ashamed that you acted so childishly. Perhaps he is right. You've never once thought of using your power for revenge, for cruelty.

"My magic actually saved our lives, didn't it?" you ask quietly.

"We didn't have a chance against all those evil goblins without it, Mialie. Not a chance."

You feel relief running through your veins now. You turn and smile at Shaw, looking into his eyes.

"All my life, Shaw," you say, "I've been afraid of my powers. Now all of a sudden . . ."

"I know, Mialie. I know."

"Sometimes I feel you know me very well," you say. "You were right about our having a lot in common."

You both sit silently for a few moments. You can feel Shaw's shoulder against yours, and the closeness gives you a glow of happiness.

Suddenly, he turns and cups your chin in his hand, brushing his thumb across your lips. A sparkle of warmth travels through you, straight to your heart.

"Mialie," he says, moving closer.

Just then you hear something. You grasp his wrist with both your hands and straighten up, saying, "Listen! Do you hear what I hear?"

Far down through the cave tunnels you hear the gritty rasping of voices, goblin voices.

"The spell has ended!" you cry. "The goblins are coming after us, Shaw!"

You both leap to your feet and dash into the far passageway, racing as fast as you can. Soon you come upon another chamber, with a big opening at the far end. You are racing straight toward it when a faint light at the side of the cave catches your eye.

"Look over there, Shaw!" The light is radiating from a small round hole at the base of the wall. "This might be a better way to go," you say. "We can be sure the goblins won't follow us anywhere there's light."

You inch your way over to the hole and peek in. You see a huge room with a man sitting cross-legged in the middle of the floor. His beard is so long it must be twice his height. He is clad in a red robe embroidered with gold and green threads, and his eyes are shut.

"I wonder what he's doing here?" whispers Shaw. "It seems very strange."

"It certainly does," you agree.

"We have no time to waste, Mialie," says Shaw. "Which way do you want to go?"

"Straight ahead through the large opening."
Turn to page 111.

"Let's go through the hole into the bearded man's chamber." *Turn to page 75.*

You move toward Shaw, and Adriana's eyes narrow in anger. In a flash, you whip Shaw's sword from its sheath and point it straight at the sprite.

"Leave him alone or I'll have your head!" you threaten, shocked by your boldness.

Instead of recoiling in fear, Adriana stares at you sweetly and begins to strum a song on Shaw's mandolin. Her eyes don't leave you for a moment, and you find yourself forgetting your anger. *She's such a lovely, harmless creature*, you think.

"Do you like my music?" she asks sweetly. "Why not lay the sword down and listen?"

You shake your head, afraid that she may be enchanting you, but your eyes cannot move from hers. It's as if they are magnetized by the deep violet color that sparkles so brightly.

Adriana looks sidelong at Shaw, beneath her feathery lashes. "Take the sword from her, sweet fighter," she croons.

Shaw moves toward you and gently pulls his sword from your hands, replacing it in his sheath. Your head is foggy, but you are vaguely aware that something is wrong.

I should try a spell to keep her from charming me, you think. *But why should I fight her? Her music is so sweet and lovely, and her eyes are like amethysts.*

Soon your mind is floating away somewhere in a dream, an amethyst dream, where you see purple rivers and violet skies, and all is peaceful . . .

THE END

You search through the pages of your spell book for the Sleep Spell, your head dizzy with magic words.

"I'll need some sand for this spell," you tell Shaw. He scrapes particles off the gritty walls of the chamber as you focus your mind on the spell.

"Once the dragon is fast asleep, we can pry his claws open and free Waldemar," you say.

"Great," says Shaw. He touches your hand as he gives you the sand, and for a moment all you can think of is the gentleness of his touch. *The spell,* you tell yourself, *think of the spell. This is no time to be distracted.*

You both creep back down the tunnel toward the dragon's lair, and soon you can see the beast shaking Waldemar in its claw with glee.

"Now stand back, Shaw," you direct. "I don't want you to be affected by this Sleep Spell."

At the sound of your voice, the dragon turns in your direction, and you cast your spell, the words spilling quickly from your mouth. But when you've finished speaking, you realize that the dragon has been mumbling words itself, and now it throws back its head, laughing wildly.

"So you thought you would put me to sleep, did you?" it howls. "I'm not as vulnerable to your tricks as you would hope! Your little spell has failed!" Its loud, cruel laughter makes you shudder, and you are now even more determined to destroy the evil creature.

Before you have time to cast another spell, the dragon opens its loathesome mouth and lunges toward you, ready to sink its huge, jagged teeth into you. Thinking quickly, you raise your arms and POOF! an invisible shield rises between you and the beast, and the monster's biting jaw smashes hard against it.

"I'll destroy you for this!" screeches the dragon, its eyes blazing with fury.

It whips its powerful tail against the invisible barrier, shattering it to bits. The tail flies toward you, and you and Shaw leap back to avoid the blow.

The beast howls in rage and lunges at you again, its teeth bared. You spin around and charge down the tunnel, Shaw right behind you. Soon you are in the next chamber again, huddled with Shaw, trying to plan your next move.

"The dragon's magic is strong," you say. "But if we catch it off guard, I could cast the Fireball Spell before it can counter with its own magic."

"You're right, Mialie," says Shaw. "It's the only option left."

Please turn to page 101.

"It's not much farther to the cavern now, Mialie," says Shaw. "Once we leave this leprechaun country, we'll be entering a dark woods along the bluff. The Cavern of Enchantment is hidden there."

You travel along the river and over the green hills all afternoon. Finally, just when the sun begins to set, you see the forest up ahead.

"We've been lucky today," you say. "No sign of leprechauns or Yorguths on our trail."

"Don't speak too soon, Mialie," says Shaw. "We're not there yet, and the woods can be very unfriendly, especially with night falling."

You trudge uphill, into the dark forest, and soon find yourself on a pass with jagged rocks walling you in on either side. Tangled evergreens cling to the rocks, their roots curling over the path. All is silent, except an owl hooting ominously in the darkness.

Feeling a shiver go up your spine, you say, "I don't like it here. Perhaps we should wait for daylight."

"Too late for that, Mialie," says Shaw, grinning. He has stopped before a great opening in the rock. The opening is overhung with concealing vines.

"It looks like the mouth of a cave," you say.

"It's the cavern, Mialie," says Shaw, "the Cavern of Enchantment!"

Your jaw drops open. "But it's dark and frightening," you say. "I expected a sort of magical place, full of crystals, maybe. Or starlight."

Just then, your gaze moves to a huge shape lying on the floor of the cavern. The moonlight shines eerily on a face, a large face with a scowling mouth, and blank, stony eyes.

"A Yorguth, Shaw!" you cry. "It's a dead Yorguth!"

Shaw draws his sword and pokes the leg of the barbarian. The tapping sound you hear is like metal on stone.

"A Yorguth turned to stone," says Shaw. "Just like the stories I've heard."

Then you see more. Statues of Yorguths lie about the cavern floor, overturned and covered with vines, their angry faces preserved forever in stone.

"Amazing, isn't it?" you murmur. "But won't we be turned to stone, too?" you ask Shaw.

"No, Mialie," he says. "Legend has it that only evil people are affected by the spell."

"I hope the legend is right," you say, slowly entering the darkness of the cavern.

You breathe a sigh of relief when you find yourself safely inside, standing in a pool of moonlight that shines through a hole in the roof.

"I feel something strange," you say. "This place is truly enchanted, it has an aura about it . . ."

Suddenly, you are silent, for as you watch, the moonlight gleams on the walls of the cavern, revealing inscriptions carved into the rocks. You look at them more closely and gasp, "It's writing, Shaw! It's Gallenian, the language that was forbidden when the Yorguths conquered the kingdom!"

"Can you read it, Mialie?" Shaw asks anxiously.

"Yes," you say. "With my powers I should be able to decipher the inscriptions."

A great rock to your left is bright with moonlight, and you touch your fingertips to the carvings, concentrating. Suddenly, the language is as clear as your own.

Your heart quickens as you read:

The Princess Maria Analie is stolen
This very day from her cradle
By Ungaar of the Yorguths.
In exchange for her life
We sacrifice ourselves and our kingdom.

"That's it, Shaw. That's all it says."

"No, Mialie, look!" cries Shaw. "There's more over here!" Shaw is pointing to another huge rock, carved with inscriptions.

You touch the next rock, reading:

Your gift, Maria Analie,
Is a power far greater than ours.
You alone can destroy the evil Ungaar
And restore freedom and goodness
To the Kingdom of Gallendale.

"Mialie," says Shaw quietly, "does the name Maria Analie sound familiar?"

You frown, searching your mind for a connection. "No . . . ," you answer, "no, it doesn't."

"But look at it more closely. It could be your birth name." He points to the letters in the name that spell Mialie: MarIA anaLIE. "And think of what the messages are saying," he continues. "A baby, stolen by Ungaar. Someone with great power. It fits, Mialie. The description fits you."

You fall into silence, unable to believe it is possible. Your eyes search the rocks for more clues. The moonlight shines on another rock at the base of the cavern wall. There is a tiny handprint embedded in the stone, and an inscription above it reads:

The Scepter of Power beneath this rock
Can be removed by one handprint alone,
That of Maria Analie.
Use its power well, Fair Princess,
That Gallendale be regained.

"It is signed 'The King and Queen of Gallendale' Shaw," you say quietly. "My parents. Can it be true?"

"Put your hand in the print," says Shaw. "Then you will know the truth."

You hold your breath and place your hand gently over the tiny handprint. Slowly the rock moves from the base of the wall, and you gasp in astonishment.

There lies the scepter, gleaming brightly, its jewels shimmering red and blue and green in the golden handle. You reach down, your heart fluttering.

Just then, a tiny voice from behind you peeps, "So you've found the Scepter of Power."

You spin around to see the goldfinch Worm hovering in the air, another scroll dangling from her beak.

"Yes, Worm," you say, still struck with wonder and disbelief.

"And now you know what the wizard Junius knew all along, Mialie," she says. "You are the rightful heir to the Kingdom of Gallendale, and you have the power to overturn the Yorguth rule."

"Yes," you say, gripping the scepter tightly. You look at the scroll in Worm's beak. "Don't tell me you're sending me on another mission already, Worm? I haven't even finished my work here yet."

"I'm not certain what this message is all about, Mialie," the finch answers. "The scroll was sent by Lord Ungaar. He's been searching night and day for you and found me over by the river. He asked me to bring it to you at once."

"You didn't tell him where I was headed, did you?" you ask.

"Of course not! I told him I wasn't sure I could even find you."

"I can imagine what it says!" mutters Shaw. "It's probably full of threats and angry warnings."

"Lord Ungaar can't hurt me anymore," you say firmly. "Now that I know the truth, his threats are meaningless."

"You don't have to read it, Mialie," says Worm. "I can always tell him I didn't find you."

"No," you say. "I'm curious to know what it says."

Worm drops the scroll into your hand. You unroll it carefully, and suddenly, your palms begin to sweat, as you wonder what awful words he has written inside.

"Read it out loud!" pipes the finch.

But you move away from Worm and Shaw, back against the rocks of the cavern. Heart pounding, you read the bold black script in Ungaar's handwriting:

My Mialie,

My heart is aching since you've left. I cannot go on without you. I have never told you my darkest secret: I love you, Mialie. I have always loved you.

I beg of you, return to me, not as my servant, but as my wife. We shall rule the Kingdoms of Gallendale and Blissford together and live in happiness for the rest of our days.

You are all I have in the world, and whatever you ask of me, that I will do. Do not turn your back on me now.

Your loving and faithful Lord,
Ungaar of the Yorguths

"No!" you gasp. You feel all color draining from your face. "I never imagined . . ." You drop the scroll to the ground and clasp both hands to your mouth.

"What is it?" cries Shaw. "What has he done to you?" Shaw reaches for the parchment, but you crush it beneath your foot before he can read it.

"It's very private," you say, your voice choking. *Perhaps Ungaar stole me from my cradle, perhaps he is an evil and cruel man,* you think. *But I never knew that deep inside, he really . . . is it possible? That he really loves me?* You remember kneeling before him, pledging your loyalty to him . . .

You shake your head, feeling confused. *How could I ever forgive him for what he's done? And yet . . . perhaps he wants to change, and my love could change him. He said he would do whatever I asked of him . . . Maybe the power of good that I have is strong enough to conquer the evil within him. To turn my back on him now would be so cruel.*

Then your eyes move to Shaw, to his fair curls and his lean body, his bright eyes, his glistening sword. You feel your heart being ripped in half, the pain too much for you to bear. You bury your face in your hands, trembling.

"You don't have to give him an answer," says Worm. She flies to your shoulder, stroking your hair with her beak. "Can I help, Mialie?"

"No, Worm," you murmur. "This is a decision I must make alone."

What are you going to do?

You will return to Ungaar, hoping that
your power will mend his evil ways.
If this is your decision, turn to page 87.

Ungaar and his Yorguths are evil; you must do
what you can to destroy them!
If you make this choice, turn to page 155.

"You are more powerful than I, Waldemar," you cry. But before you can ask the wizard to cast a spell, Shaw leaps toward Ungaar, and with a powerful thrust, plunges his sword through the overlord's heart. Ungaar howls in pain and horror and slumps forward, falling into the cavern. Instantly, his body is turned to a crumpled heap of stone.

At the sight of Ungaar turning to stone, the other Yorguths cry out in fright, and scatter through the woods, fearful of their own fates.

"A just end to an evil man," says Waldemar. "And all credit goes to Shaw, King of Blissford. It is he who is responsible for this great triumph of good over evil."

The wizard turns toward you. At that very moment, the scepter moves slowly from your hands and resumes its place at the base of the cavern wall. The rock embedded with the handprint slides over it, locking the scepter away.

"The power was given to you, Mialie," says the wizard, "and you did not accept it. The scepter knows that you are not yet ready to rule the Kingdom of Gallendale."

You close your eyes, and a great surge of darkness overwhelms you, as if you have been stripped of all happiness.

"And now I can no longer fulfill my destiny," you say emptily.

"No, Mialie. Your destiny is not lost to you," says Waldemar, wrapping his arm around you. "You are merely struggling. The power will always be there. It will wait for you."

"But what shall I do in the meantime?" you cry.

"First, you must trust that the power will return.

Second, you must learn all you can about the magic that is within you. I will help you. I will teach you everything I know. One day, a great light will fill your heart, and you will know that you are ready to return to the cavern and accept the power you have inherited."

You look over at Shaw, who is watching you with gentle eyes.

"And you are now King of Blissford, Shaw," you say. "Will you remember me when you are grandly famous, a fine king whose name is known throughout the kingdom?"

Shaw moves toward you and cups your face in his hands. "Remember you?" he asks. "How could I ever forget you, Mialie?"

"I feel very forgettable at the moment," you say.

"Mialie," he says, pulling you toward him. "I must ask you something. When you are ready to rule Gallendale, perhaps . . ." He looks into your eyes.

"Yes?"

"Perhaps you will consider uniting our kingdoms, ruling as the King and Queen of Gallenford . . ."

"Shaw," you say slowly, thoughtfully. "I need time before I can answer you. I'm not saying 'no,' but I need more time. First I must accept myself and my gifts, and only then will I be able to consider more. Can you understand?"

"Perfectly," he says, smiling. "And I give you this promise: I will be here when you have completed your work. I will wait for you, Mialie, whether it takes a week or a month or a lifetime. I will wait until you are ready."

Shaw bends to kiss your forehead. The tenderness of his touch sends a glow through you, comforting the heaviness and pain in your heart. You slip your arms around his waist and bury your head in his chest.

"Oh, Shaw," you say. "I was so close to accepting my powers. So close . . ."

He holds you tightly, stroking your hair over and over. "That's why it won't be long before we are together again, Mialie. You must believe that."

And deep in your heart, you do believe it. You know that soon you will be at the end of this quest, holding the Scepter of Power in your hand. And then you will be ready to begin a new journey and rule the Kingdom of Gallenford, with Shaw forever at your side.

THE END

"Farewell, Shaw of Blissford," you say quietly. "Perhaps I shall meet you again someday."

"Perhaps," says Shaw. He pauses for a moment, as if he wants to say more.

"Perhaps you will come across the pearl one day and rule the Kingdom of Blissford," you add.

"Perhaps," he answers. Then he reaches up and brushes your cheek with the back of his hand. "Fare-

well, Mialie. Godspeed," he says and strides off into the moonlight. You hear his footsteps grow fainter and fainter, until, finally, they are gone.

You turn away slowly, your eyes blurred with tears, and pick up your scepter. It is time to go to your parents' castle and begin your reign.

THE END

"Shaw," you say gently, "if I stayed here with you, I would always be plagued with doubts about my decision. I feel there is something important waiting for me at the cavern, and I must find out what it is."

Shaw nods his head slowly. "I understand, Mialie. And if you find what you are looking for at the cavern, perhaps we still can come back and live here."

"Perhaps," you answer.

"Let's get some rest here tonight, Mialie," he says. "Then we'll be fresh when we start out in the morning. It's been quite a day, hasn't it?"

"It certainly has been, Shaw," you agree. You curl up next to the hearth and drop off to sleep instantly.

The next thing you know, it is morning. The sunlight streams through the splintered windows, and you jump up, full of energy.

Shaw is already downstairs in the entrance chamber, waiting for you.

"Let's go, Mialie," he says brightly. "We'll be heading out of the woods across some beautiful hills today. I think you'll like it."

Behind the castle, you pass through a grove of aspen trees, and Shaw reaches up to grab hold of a limb. "I spent many days climbing in these trees," he says, swinging himself on an aspen branch.

He lands gracefully, and then, as you watch, your eyes widen in shock. Shaw floats into the air and stays there as if held up by a magical force.

In a flash, his sword slides from its sheath and flies through the aspens, vanishing out across the hills.

"Put me down, blast you!" Shaw growls, angrier than you have ever seen him. "And return my sword to me this very instant!"

For a moment, you think Shaw is addressing you, but before you can open your mouth to speak, a playful voice comes from high in the treetops. "What sword? I don't see anything in that sheath of yours, do you?"

"Thanks to you, it's empty!" snarls Shaw. "Now stop playing your silly games and show yourself now!"

"At your service," pipes a voice beside you, and suddenly, POOF! Emerald sparks fly from the forest floor, and a band of leprechauns appears, all dancing on the tips of their toes. Their eyes twinkle with mischief, the tassels of their cocked hats bounce gaily.

"Might you be obliging enough to set me down?" asks Shaw.

The little men who are carrying him wink at each other and release Shaw, sending him to the ground with a PLOP.

"Thank you kindly," says Shaw, rubbing his back as he sits up.

A rosy-cheeked leprechaun leaps down from a tree and bends over Shaw. He puffs on a gnarled pipe, blowing colorful smoke rings in Shaw's face.

"And might you like a stool to sit on while we talk?" he quips. In a flash, a toadstool beneath Shaw turns into a fine wooden stool.

"There, now," pipes the leprechaun. "Isn't that a bit more comfortable?"

"Comfort does not interest me at the moment," says Shaw. "My sword does. And I demand that you return it immediately."

"Now why on earth would I want to do that?" asks the leprechaun, twiddling with his pipe.

"Because if you don't, my friend Mialie here will see to it that you are turned into a toadstool in no time flat!" Shaw grabs for the creature, catching him in his hand, but with a sparkling POOF! the leprechaun vanishes and reappears on an aspen branch.

"I wouldn't suggest threats," says the little man, winking. "No, that won't do at all. Not at all."

Shaw slumps back down on the stool. Tiny leprechaun hands wriggle through his pockets, snatching out pieces of gold. The creatures leap about, tossing the golden coins in the air with glee.

"Then just what is it you would suggest?" Shaw asks with barely concealed anger.

"Oh, dear," says the leprechaun in the tree, rubbing his chin with his hand. "Let me think."

Suddenly his eyes gleam with an idea. "Those gold pieces of yours must have come from a pot somewhere," he says. "You get us that pot of gold, and you shall have your sword back sooner than you can say 'Rainbow's End.' "

Shaw's eyes cloud over, but your mind is spinning quickly. *Perhaps something in Shaw's knapsack could be transformed to look like gold,* you think. *I wonder if they would fall for such a trick?*

"Take me to wherever it is that you have sent my sword, and I shall tell you where to find your pot of gold," says Shaw, bluffing.

"Your sword is in our lair," says the leprechaun. "We will take you there, but the sword will not be back in your hands until the pot of gold is in ours."

Shaw shoots a determined look at you. You know he intends to grab his sword and run from the lair.

I wonder if it would be safer to avoid entering the lair—anything could happen there, you think. *Perhaps the spell is a better idea.*

You must make your decision quickly. You have two choices:

You can follow Shaw's plan and head for the leprechaun's lair. *Turn to page 95.*

Or you can cast a Fool's Gold Spell. *Turn to page 121.*

You turn around, pretending to leave the room, and open your book so Adriana cannot see. "Ray of Enfeeblement," you read. "A good spell to reduce her charms."

Adriana is just slipping Shaw's mandolin from his shoulder, enticing him to play for her, when you spin around and FLASH! You shoot a flaming green ray of light at her.

For a moment she stands still, stunned from the light, and then she continues her train of thought.

"Play an ode to beauty for me, sweet fighter," she says, placing the mandolin in Shaw's hands. He takes his instrument and flings it back over his shoulder.

"I haven't the time," he says, nicely but firmly. "Mialie and I must be on our way."

You breathe a sigh of relief and smile brightly at the sprite. Her violet eyes glare back at you.

"But we must be alone," she tells Shaw. "My marvels are for your eyes only."

Shaw takes the flower from his hair and hands it to her. "I'm sorry," he says, "but I must leave."

And with that, he walks over to you and takes your hand. You make your way down the wooden ladder and out the door. As you step outside, Adriana is crooning from the window: "Come back, young fighter. Don't leave me all alone. I have such wonders . . ."

But you are beyond the stand of oaks now, and her voice fades away behind you.

"What was that green light, Mialie?" Shaw asks.

"Light?" you say innocently. "What light?" You feel this spell best be kept a secret.

Shaw shakes his head. "Never mind. My head feels a little foggy."

You smile a secretive smile. "How much farther will we be traveling?" you ask, wanting to change the subject.

"We're very close now," says Shaw. "We just have to get to those bluffs ahead."

"Let's hurry!" you urge. "I can't wait to get to the cavern!"

The two of you race through the grass until you are surrounded by the dark trees that edge a steep bluff.

Shaw begins climbing the bluff, and you follow, using tree roots to get your footing. Night is falling, and all is silent except the hooting of a distant owl. Moonbeams flicker through the rustling leaves above, lighting your way.

You both make your way along the bluff pass, jagged rocks walling you in on either side, until you come upon an enormous opening in the rocks on your right.

In the moonlight you can make out the dark mouth of a cave, half-hidden by overhanging vines.

"Can this be it, Shaw?" you cry, your heart racing. "Is this the Cavern of Enchantment?"

Then you stop, frozen in your tracks. Moonlight shines within, illuminating a figure with a huge head and wild hair. It is a Yorguth, his blank eyes staring out at you from the blackness of the cavern. You hear the scrape of metal as Shaw slowly draws his sword from its sheath. He has seen it, too, and you both back down toward the bluff trail.

Suddenly, Shaw chuckles under his breath.

"It's a Yorguth, all right, Mialie," he says, approaching the barbarian and poking him with his blade. "A Yorguth turned to stone."

Then you see more. There are ten, maybe twenty

Yorguths lying on the ground by the cavern, hidden between the rocks and tree roots, all perfect stone statues.

"Do you think it's safe for us to enter?" you ask Shaw, as he makes his way toward the cavern. "According to legend, the spell only affects those who are evil," Shaw explains.

Barely breathing, you and Shaw enter the cavern and sigh with relief when you stand inside, unharmed.

"Look!" says Shaw, pointing to a small opening in the roof of the cavern. As you watch through the hole, the full moon gradually rises directly overhead, flooding the cavern with its light.

"Look at the stones on the wall here," whispers Shaw. "They have some kind of message on them!"

In the light of the full moon, inscriptions have appeared, hewn into the rock. You stand still and watch, as if just for you, the secrets of the cavern unfold.

"The writing is Gallenian, Shaw," you say. "I thought all Gallenian records were destroyed when the Yorguths executed the royalty of Gallendale."

"So did I," says Shaw in amazement. "Can you use your powers to decipher the messages, Mialie?"

"I'll try, Shaw," you say, touching your fingers to one of the rocks. Suddenly, the carved inscription is clear as your own language, and you read the writing aloud:

The Princess Maria Analie is stolen
This very day from her cradle
By Ungaar of the Yorguths.
In exchange for her life

We sacrifice ourselves and our kingdom.
Your gift, Maria Analie,
Is a power far greater than ours.
You alone can destroy the evil Ungaar
And restore freedom and goodness
To the Kingdom of Gallendale.

You fall into silence. *Ungaar, stealing a tiny princess from her own parents,* you think. *He is more wicked than I even imagined.*

"But what does all this have to do with me?" you say out loud.

Shaw is frowning, as if lost in thought. "I think it's beginning to make sense," he says. "Keep reading, Mialie. There's another message down there."

You look to where Shaw is pointing and see a rock embedded with a tiny handprint. The inscription above it reads:

The Scepter of Power beneath this rock
Can be removed by one handprint alone:
That of Maria Analie.
Use its power well, fair Princess,
That Gallendale be regained.

"It is signed 'The King and Queen of Gallendale,' " you say quietly. "But I still don't understand, Shaw. Why have I been sent to read these messages? I don't know where to find this Maria Analie . . ."

"I think you do, Mialie," says Shaw. "I think they're talking about you. You are Maria Analie."

"No!" you gasp. You read the messages again, unable to believe it is possible. "Could I . . ." you say

at last, "could I truly be of noble parentage?"

"Move your hand to the print, and we'll see." says Shaw.

You take a deep breath and place your hand gently over the tiny handprint, your heart quickening, and very slowly, the rock moves from the base of the cavern, revealing a golden rod, gleaming with jewels of red and blue and green. It is the Scepter of Power.

You reach down, and just before you grasp it in your hand, a voice behind you bellows, "Stop!"

You spin around and stand face-to-face with Ungaar, "You are a fool, child," he sneers. "An utter fool!" The fire of his eyes burns through you.

"Touch that scepter, and you shall be turned to stone forever!" he snarls.

I will not let him destroy me, you think. *The power*

has been given to me, and now I shall never let him take it away. You raise your chin in defiance.

"That is a lie," you say. "I know the truth now, Ungaar, and the scepter is rightfully mine."

A burst of cruel laughter spills from his mouth. "You believe the inscriptions you have found, my foolish child? You don't think others before you have found these messages of sorcery, all woven to trick them into touching the scepter? Ha!" he laughs. "How naive you are to be deceived by the magic messages!"

You feel your hands begin to shake. "Do not let him influence you," says Shaw. "Take the scepter into your hands and accept the power given you."

You stare boldly into Ungaar's crazed eyes. "I shall no longer be deceived by you," you say.

You reach down and take the scepter into your hands. A sudden glow radiates all around you, filling the cavern with a great green light.

You hold the scepter high. "Soon goodness shall prevail in the Kingdom of Gallendale," you say.

With a raging bellow, Ungaar lunges at you with his dagger. Instinctively, you point the scepter at him.

A bolt of lightning shoots from the scepter toward the dagger, stopping it in midair. The dagger turns and plunges itself deep into Ungaar's heart. He howls in anguish, screaming, "Traitor! Sorceress!"

He staggers into the cavern, his hands reaching toward you as if he wants to rip you limb from limb. You stand firm, your heart pounding wildly, and watch as he turns to stone. A sudden, complete silence engulfs the cavern.

"Justice prevails," says Shaw quietly. "If the Yorguths have no leader, they have no power."

You tighten your grip on the scepter, and a strange feeling surges through your veins. You are the ruler of the kingdom, but you are not frightened. You understand your power at last, and you accept it.

Shaw moves toward you, slipping his sword back into its sheath. "You used your powers well, Mialie," he says. "I am certain you will make a just queen."

"I shall do my best," you say, awed to hear your title for the first time.

You look at Shaw, and he seems melancholy, his eyes a deep gray. "I'd say you've accomplished more than you ever dreamed of, Mialie." He hesitates, as if he wants to ask you something. "Even though you are Queen of Gallendale now . . ." he begins.

"Yes, Shaw?"

But he shakes his head, as if he cannot continue. "Well," he says finally, "I suppose it's time I was off in search of my own dream again. You have found your scepter, Maria Analie, and it's time I found my pearl."

Pain stabs your heart. *He can't really be leaving!* you think. *Can't I help him find his dream, now that he has helped me find mine?*

You want so badly to ask him to stay. *But what if he says 'no'?* you think. *What if he's not in love with me after all?*

You have one final decision to make, and you must make it now.

If you decide to be bold and ask Shaw to stay and rule the kingdom with you, turn to page 78.

If you want to let him go his own way now, hoping he will return someday, turn to page 140.

You close your eyes, concentrating. A great warmth surges through you, and you lift the scepter high, pointing it directly at Ungaar. You open your eyes.

"May Gallendale be regained!" you cry.

Instantly, a tremendous bolt of lightning flashes from the sceptor and strikes the overlord's heart, igniting his body in a blaze of green fire.

"Sorceress!" howls Ungaar. "You have betrayed me!" But his body is shrinking before your eyes, consumed by the powerful flames of magic. Soon the cries weaken and die away, and a smoldering pile of ashes lies where Ungaar had stood.

Witnessing the end of their leader, the Yorguths scatter through the woods, screaming in terror.

"Now justice shall prevail," says Waldemar, bowing to you. "I am deeply humbled to see such great power handled with the confidence of a master. You deserve my respect."

You let out a sigh of relief. You feel calm and strong, all trace of fear has fled.

"And now you are Queen of Gallendale," says Shaw, crossing to your side. He wraps his arm around your shoulder and pulls you close. "How does it feel?"

"It feels right," you say quietly. You look up at him. "And you, Shaw, you are King of Blissford."

"Yes," he says. "And soon the Kingdoms of Gallendale and Blissford will be renowned for their just and good leadership."

"You're not going to keep separate kingdoms, are you?" cries Waldemar. "Why not unite them? Why not establish one great kingdom, the Kingdom of Gallenford?"

Shaw's eyes fill with brightness and joy, and he

cups your face in his hands. "Why not?" he asks. "What do you think, Mialie? With our combined strength, our power would be greater still."

You smile up at him. "I think that's a splendid idea . . . King Shaw and Queen Mialie of Gallenford," you say, relishing the sounds of your new titles.

"It does sound nice, doesn't it?" says Shaw quietly. He leans down, his face close to yours. You can feel the warmth and softness of his breath on your cheek, and your heart glows. Then he brushes his lips on yours and kisses you gently.

"And so it's done!" cries Waldemar. "And I'd say this occasion calls for a special display of starlight!"

With a great sweep of his arms, Waldemar shoots his stars to the roof of the cavern. In a flash, POOF! the wizard has disappeared, and you raise your heads to look at the stars.

They are clustered together, forming a heart.

You hear Waldemar's voice echo throughout the cavern: "May the heavens smile upon your dreams, and may your hearts be filled with magic."

THE END

You drag yourself up on all fours, your head spinning from the blow. The goblins, spears and swords flying, are preoccupied with Shaw now.

You creep across the dank floor toward a dead goblin. Slowly, you reach for its sword and grip it tightly, pushing yourself to your feet. You feel weak and your vision is blurred.

I must do this, you tell yourself. *If I don't fight them off, then all is lost.* You lift the sword high above your head, your arms trembling, and with all the strength you can muster, you run toward a goblin and strike it from behind. Triumphantly, you watch it tumble to the ground.

As you look toward Shaw, he is struck in the head by a goblin, and he slumps to the floor in a silken heap.

"Shaw!" you scream. But you have no time to worry about him, for now the goblins are rushing at you. The creatures growl, and you whip your sword wildly at them, knocking two more to the ground.

There are just three goblins left, and you hear their gritty voices croaking loudly through the fuzzy blur in your head.

"We've got them now!" grunts one.

"Just knock out the girl, and we'll haul them back to the lair!" croaks another.

I should have cast the Light Spell, you think, your head cloudy with dizziness. *If I can concentrate hard enough, there may still be time . . .*

But as you search your mind for the magic words, you feel a sharp blow on your forehead, and you sink to the floor, all thoughts obliterated by darkness.

THE END

"This message does not deserve an answer," you tell Worm. *There was a time when Ungaar held me in the palm of his hand,* you think. *But that time is gone. I am finished with him and his wicked ways. Besides,* you say to yourself, glancing at Shaw, *my heart lies elsewhere.*

Worm flies to perch on the scepter. "I'm so proud of you, Mialie. I know you will destroy the evil Yorguths and return justice to our kingdom," she says. "And I have a request to make."

"Anything," you answer. "After all, if it weren't for you, I may never have set off on this journey."

"I'd like to be your familiar, Mialie," she peeps, her feathers all flutter. "I can deliver magic messages for you, handle spy missions, be your guard."

"Why, I'd be delighted to have you as my familiar, Worm," you say. You turn to look at Shaw. He is kneeling at the place where the scepter was found, reaching behind the rock.

"It's here," he whispers, barely breathing. "The pearl was here with the scepter. Your parents must have protected it from Yorguth hands."

He draws his hand from the opening, and between his fingers, he holds a great, bright pearl. He sets it into the handle of his sword, and a soft green light glows around it.

He looks up at you, his eyes filled with brightness and joy.

"At last, Mialie," he says, rising to his feet. "I have found the pearl at last."

"And now you are King Shaw of Blissford," you say. "And a fine and just ruler you will be."

Shaw's eyes grow soft, and he looks at you

intently. "I believe those words, Mialie," he says. "I believe I have the power to rule with fairness and kindness. A short while ago, I didn't understand myself enough to be worthy of my calling. But because of . . ." His voice trails off.

"Because of what, Shaw?" you ask.

"Because of you, Mialie, I have become free to be myself. My search for the pearl was half-hearted, my fear of power led me to wander about aimlessly. But you have given me the strength I needed to accept my destiny."

"You have given me that same strength, Shaw," you say. "I used to think my magic was a secret, evil force lurking deep within me. Now I know that it is I who control my powers. They do not control me."

Shaw's hands grasp your shoulders and he looks at you solemnly, almost desperately.

"Then rule with me, Mialie," he says. "We can help each other through the difficult times ahead, trying to restore order where there is chaos, good where there is evil."

"I will, Shaw," you answer, glowing. "We will build a great castle over the Cavern of Enchantment and rule together, as King and Queen of Gallendale."

He leans toward you and kisses you then, long and gently. A joyous warmth fills your heart. You throw your arms around his neck, hugging him tightly.

"The kingdom will be better for our reign," says Shaw.

"Yes," you say, full of hope and determination. "For we will be true to ourselves."

THE END

ENDLESS QUEST™ Books

From the producers of the DUNGEONS & DRAGONS® Game

#1 DUNGEON OF DREAD
#2 MOUNTAIN OF MIRRORS
#3 PILLARS OF PENTEGARN
#4 RETURN TO BROOKMERE
#5 REVOLT OF THE DWARVES
#6 REVENGE OF THE RAINBOW DRAGONS
#7 HERO OF WASHINGTON SQUARE
based on the TOP SECRET® Game
#8 VILLAINS OF VOLTURNUS
based on the STAR FRONTIERS™ Game
#9 ROBBERS AND ROBOTS
based on the TOP SECRET® Game
#10 CIRCUS OF FEAR
#11 SPELL OF THE WINTER WIZARD
#12 LIGHT ON QUESTS MOUNTAIN
based on the GAMMA WORLD® Game
#13 DRAGON OF DOOM
#14 RAID ON NIGHTMARE CASTLE

For a free catalog, write:
TSR, Inc.
P.O. Box 756, Dept. EQB
Lake Geneva, WI 53147

The World's Most Talked About Role-Playing Game

Our DUNGEONS & DRAGONS® game is the best way to enter the world of role-playing. And now the Basic Set is even easier to play. Send for your FREE color poster/catalog today:

TSR Hobbies, Inc.
Box 756, C188EQB
Lake Geneva, WI 53147

In the UK:
TSR Hobbies, (UK) Ltd.
The Mill, Rathmore Rd.
Cambridge, ENGLAND
CB1 4AD

TSR, Inc.
PRODUCTS OF YOUR IMAGINATION™